CHOKE POINT

Also by James C. Mitchell

Lovers Crossing

CHOKE POINT

James C. Mitchell

St. Martin's Minotaur
New York

 For information, address St. Martin's Press, 175 Fifth Avenue, New York, N.Y. 10010.

www.minotaurbooks.com

Library of Congress Cataloging-in-Publication Data

Mitchell, James C. (James Craig), 1942–
Choke point / James C. Mitchell.—1st St. Martin's Minotaur ed.
p. cm.
ISBN 0-312-31532-5
EAN 978-0312-31532-0
1. Private investigators—Arizona—Fiction. 2. Women journalists—Crimes against—Fiction. 3. Mexican-American Border Region—Fiction. 4. Americans—Mexico—Fiction. 5. Arizona—Fiction. 6. Mexico—Fiction. I. Title.

PS3613.I855C47 2004
813'.6—dc22

2004049401

First Edition: October 2004

10 9 8 7 6 5 4 3 2 1

For the Franklin Gang

A dog starved at his master's gate
Predicts the ruin of the state.

—William Blake,
"Auguries of Innocence"

CHOKE POINT

CHAPTER 1

THREE DAYS BEFORE THE FIRST MURDER, SAL GARCIA SAID, "YOU want to go to a riot?"

We were in U-Needa-Bebida, downtown. It was a late Friday afternoon in Tucson's early spring. A few drinkers hung around in the dim barroom, supposedly waiting for rush-hour traffic to thin out. We sat back in worn brown leather chairs at the bar where our fathers had bought each other beers on afternoons like this. I had a Negra Modelo and Sal had a Coors. Norah Jones and Lalo Guerrero took turns on the CD changer.

"What riot?" I asked.

"The riot we're having on Monday night," Sal said. "After the game."

"The truth comes out," I said. "You guys plan these things in advance to spike the ratings."

Sal shoots video for a Tucson newscast. He's in his mid-forties and thinks of himself as a geezer in a kids' game. Sometimes he really does seem to know the news before it happens.

"No planning required, Brinker," he said. "We got to the Final Four in '97 and won, and there was a riot. We played in '01 and lost, and there was a riot. We're a cinch to make the championship game on Monday night, so guess what? Win or lose, the Old Pueblo's rumbling."

Sal said "we" the way everyone in Tucson talks about University of Arizona teams.

"Not this year," I told him. "The cops say they've learned from their mistakes."

"Yeah, right," Sal said.

"They're turning out in force. They canceled all their vacations and days off."

"Sure."

"Everything will be under control this time. I saw that on your news, in fact."

Sal laughed and said, "You *believe* our news?"

SO ON THAT MONDAY NIGHT IN EARLY APRIL, SAL AND I CLIMBED the creaky wooden stairs of the former movie theater on Fourth Avenue. He had been right. Arizona won Saturday's game, knocking off a tenth seed that somehow lucked into the Final Four. The UA would play Duke for the championship.

At the top of the stairs, we stepped outside onto the roof. Sal carried his video camera and tripod and a small television monitor. I lugged his big aluminum case, padded inside, filled with heavy gear and extra tapes. *That's* why he asked me along, I thought. Or maybe he just wanted to hear something about Dolores.

At eight-thirty, the night was cool and full dark except for streetlights and a kaleidoscopic neon glow from the avenue's bar windows. The police helicopter made slow, noisy passes above. A slim slice of moon sprinkled faint light onto the side streets and alleys. It wasn't much, though. All I could see in the residential section were shadowy figures moving about. Some emerged to the relative brightness of the avenue. Others vanished into yards or doorways or simply walked into the darker distance.

Two floors down and to our right, the student saloon district bustled. It was a basic college business block. By day, you found funky clothing shops, a feminist bookstore, cheap eats. At night, the bars ruled. This evening, kids partied from one to another. They showed ID to the bouncers and hurried inside. Sounds of laughter and whiffs of marijuana drifted up to the rooftop. Every so often, I heard a cheer when Arizona hit a basket or a groan when Duke scored. It seemed almost innocent. A festive game night in a college town.

Almost.

The police command post, a huge, martial RV in black and white, hunkered down on our left. Two hundred officers, I guessed, massed around it. They were putting on their helmets and bulletproof vests, and testing the heft of clear, hard plastic shields that would protect them from head to thigh. Several cops walked a few steps forward and a few steps back, then did it again, rehearsing some weird urban disorder suppression dance known only to them. A few thwacked their riot clubs into leather-gloved hands.

Sal held out his arms to indicate our supposedly safe rooftop.

"The value of seniority," he said. He walked to the edge and tossed two cables down to a news van parked at the curb. "Rick Keene and Benny Quijano, the new guys, they're on the street. Right in the middle of it when the head-busting starts."

At the command post, a tall cop with sergeant's stripes was getting the troops lined up. They stood in close ranks, about twenty to a row across the avenue, two blocks north of the bars.

"First thing to watch for," Sal said, "is when some girl sits on a guy's shoulders, big crowd around yelling at her, and she pulls up her shirt to show her tits. That's when you know the mob is well lubricated and ready to rock. I like to get that shot."

"Sure, I'll watch for that," I said.

"Knew I could count on you," Sal said.

"Can you actually use that video?" I asked him, laughing.

"Not on the air," he said, "but we'll put it in the gag reel for the station Christmas party."

Sal stood close to the edge of the roof and surveyed the scene below.

"Everybody knows what's going to happen tonight except those poor devils," he said, pointing to the police. "They think they have a plan. Yeah, right."

He stood aside from the camera. "Look through here," he said.

I bent to peer through his viewfinder. The night exposure gave everything a pixilated, dark orange hue. Streetlights, the brightest images, bloomed in the lens like tracer fire.

"It looks like some third-world uprising on CNN," I said. "Live, from the roof of the Tegucigalpa Hilton."

"The students over here, and the junta over there," Sal said. "Great TV, guaranteed."

"And the press in the middle." I pointed to a cluster of reporters standing on the sidewalk outside O'Rourke's, one of the biggest bars. I recognized two newspaper writers and three attractive youngsters from the television stations.

The men seemed to be helping a woman I had not seen in town before. She was young and slender, like the television people, but dressed down like the newspaper types. Her back was turned to me. I couldn't see her face. Her short blond hair shone in the street lamps' glow.

The other reporters pointed to spots along the street. They gestured to indicate how the police might move toward the bars. The woman scribbled in one of those familiar notebooks that reporters use, skinny enough to shove in a pocket. When she turned, I could see that she kept brushing a bit of hair behind her right ear.

"Who's that?" I asked Sal. He was watching her, too.

"April Lennox," he said. "SNC. Southwest News Consortium from Los Angeles. They write for a bunch of alt-weeklies."

"She came all the way from L.A. to see some drunks go nuts after a basketball game?"

Sal laughed and pointed to the cops. "Good old police brutality is in the air, amigo. SNC, that's their kind of headline."

"You know her?"

"She was at the news conference down at headquarters yesterday. The one where the chief said everything will be fine tonight. All us guys introduced ourselves to her."

"A little young for you, Sal?"

"The hope lives on, the dream shall never die," he said. "How's Dolores?"

"Still in New York," I told him. He knew enough to let it go.

Sal's two-way radio crackled. He put in an earpiece, fiddled with a button, and said, "Go." After a moment, "Okay."

He bent to his camera and panned from the cops to the bars and back. "Like this?" he said, then panned twice more. "Okay, good."

He turned to me. "That was the control truck. Sometimes in these night shoots, it's hard to see when we pan. You lose the image if you go too fast."

I nodded as if I knew what he was talking about.

"Five minutes to play," I said, looking at the game on the little TV. "If something's going to pop, it'll be soon."

Down below, almost everyone had decided where to be for the big finish. The fun-seekers were on the avenue or in the bars. Neighbors along the side streets got away from the crowd, into their homes, in front of their televisions. Only one man, a short, thin fellow in jeans and a white T-shirt, stood in the dim light of an alley. He looked around nervously, perhaps uncertain about venturing into the crowd. I didn't think anything more about him. The action would be on the avenue.

With 4:23 remaining, score tied, Arizona's star guard, DeShawn Nzuma, took a charge, but got called for a blocking foul. It was his fifth, knocking him out of the game. From the tinny TV speaker, I heard Billy Packer shout, "Oh, terrible call!"

Angry roars burst from the bars. Someone threw a beer bottle. It shattered on the sidewalk. Kids poured into the street. At the command post, the sergeant pointed a bullhorn at his cops. I couldn't hear over the noise of the swelling crowd, but the cops stood a little taller, tightened their ranks, and raised the plastic shields.

In a few places, for a few moments, it looked like the goofy college drunk that Sal had predicted. Two young women pulled up their T-shirts as the crowds cheered.

But then five muscular guys, stripped to the waist, jumped on an old Volvo sedan parked around the corner from Borracho's Bar. Another kid ran up with a baseball bat and smashed the car's windows. The gang rolled the car onto its roof and danced on the exposed undercarriage.

"Now, that's entertainment!" Sal said, his eye to the viewfinder, his tape rolling. "Brink, watch for fires or kids trashing the shops. This isn't gonna stop. We'll be on live real quick here."

As if waiting for the photographer's cue, two young men picked up a big wood-framed sign from the sidewalk in front of a clothing store. They lifted the sign over their heads and heaved it through the store's big window. The plate glass shattered. The men pumped their fists. Then they looked down the street, saw another sidewalk sign, and raced toward it.

A crowd assaulted an ancient Ford pickup truck that was parked by the hot dog stand. They rolled it over and laughed as someone threw a flaming newspaper into the passenger compartment. The old upholstery caught fire as quickly as desert brush in a dry summer. The crowd cheered.

Now they had the cops' attention. The police trotted one block south, closer to the trouble, and re-formed their tight ranks.

The sergeant with the bullhorn stood in front of the officers' formation, facing the crowd.

"Attention!" he said. "This is the Tucson Police Department. This gathering is an unlawful assembly. This is an official police order to disperse. In the name of the people of the state of Arizona, I order you to leave this area immediately. Listen to me!" The crowd jeered, hundreds of voices mocking the cops.

The sergeant repeated his order. A few of the throng drifted away to parking lots or side streets. Two hundred young people faced two hundred cops, with only one long block of Fourth Avenue between them.

Turning back to the officers, the sergeant barked a command. In unison, the cops raised their clubs and tapped the sides of the big plastic shields. They slow-marched down the avenue, tapping with each step in an eerie tattoo that echoed off the storefronts.

I looked at Sal's TV monitor. The game clock clicked down to zero. Arizona lost by three. The network showed the Dukies celebrating and the Wildcats slumping at their bench. Sal's station immediately cut away from the network to local coverage from the avenue.

Saloon patrons, watching the news, saw what was happening outside. They abandoned their drinks and their bar bills and spilled into the street. By then, I knew, the cops were within range for their "less lethal weapons," tear gas and beanbags filled with tiny plastic balls like big BBs.

"A reporter got killed in L.A. in the seventies by a tear gas grenade," Sal said, never looking away from scene. "The guy was sitting in some bar, trying to stay out of trouble, and the cops shot a grenade through the window. Hit the guy right on the noggin. Keep your head down when they march by here, Brinker."

Even now, like Sal, I could see how it would unfold. The hooligans and vandals had done their damage and taken off. The guys who rolled the cars and trashed the stores were long gone. They probably weren't even college students, but just punks who used the game as an excuse to smash something. I had watched them run to the end of the street and vanish into the grimy neighborhood near the railroad tracks. The police were pouring all their force and firepower into a showdown with blotto college kids, innocent shop owners and bar bouncers, and the idiot Lookie Lou's who always showed up to gawk at trouble.

Shots sounded as the marching cops covered the first block. Not the crack of gunshots, but the thump of tear gas grenades and beanbags being fired. I barely heard them over the shouts of the crowd and the noisy march of the police. You could have fired a cannon in the nearby residential streets and nobody on the avenue would have noticed.

A couple of drunks walked toward the advancing cops, arms held out. One of them took a beanbag in the belly and went down, hollering in pain. His friend turned and ran.

That threatening drumbeat, clubs on plastic shields, droned on as the line of uniforms pushed steadily down the avenue.

The first hit of tear gas terrified the crowd. People on the edges of the cloud bolted to side streets and alleys. The unfortunate group stuck in the middle waited until the gas lifted a bit. The police fired more beanbags even before the cluster of targets was visible.

The small man in the white T-shirt finally realized what was happening on the avenue. He turned and walked quickly away, into the neighborhood. I saw him look over his shoulder just before he left the light and stepped into the shadows.

Sal Garcia kept pulling back from his viewfinder to eyeball the wider scene. He would spot some action, twist his camera on its tripod, and zoom in.

Two cops had cornered a man who failed to move out of a doorway. They whacked him with their clubs and left him there. Another man, halfway down the block, was writhing and holding his left thigh. I couldn't tell if these were good guys or bad.

Officers had cuffed three young men. I watched the police drag the shirtless men back toward the command post. Blood dripped from the forehead of one arrestee. Another shouted obscenities loud enough for us to hear on the rooftop.

Then, as if some unseen sound technician's hand had slowly turned down the volume, the din below diminished. The cops broke off their marching drumbeat. People stopped screaming as the avenue cleared. Wisps of tear gas drifted in the chill night air. I heard bits of sobbing from the street, the faint crackle of police radios, a siren far away.

A car engine started. The sound jarred me. That's how quiet the avenue had become. A block and a half away, headlights came on. I watched a white Jeep Cherokee swing into the street, then stop suddenly. In the beam of the vehicle's headlights, someone lay sprawled across the center line on the pavement. It was a slender figure, a man, I thought, wearing blue jeans and a white T-shirt stained red.

A woman jumped from the driver's side and ran to the injured man. She had not hit him. He lay in the path of her vehicle as she was about to pull out of her driveway. The woman carried a cell phone. I could see her punch at it three times as she knelt at his side. Nine-one-one, I guessed, and help would be on the way. But the victim's stillness, lying there in the glare of the Good Samaritan's headlights, told me that help would be too late.

CHAPTER 2

When I arrived at the Alejandro & Katz office on Wednesday morning, a woman stood at the receptionist's desk with her back to me. She wore loose-fitting tan slacks and a blue broadcloth shirt. A bulky purse with a long strap hung from her left shoulder. She was brushing a bit of blond hair behind her right ear.

Lupita, the receptionist, said, "Oh, here he is now."

"April Lennox," I said, as the blond woman turned around.

"Wow," she said. "You really do detect."

I laughed. "Someone pointed you out to me at the riot."

"I'm from Los Angeles," she said. "I'm not sure that Monday night qualifies as a riot."

"We're a simple people here in the boonies, but we try," I said. "Come on back."

I led her down the hall, past the lawyers' spacious office suites, to my own little investigator's garret. David Katz and Rubén

Alejandro let me use a small room in their law firm building even when I wasn't working for them. April Lennox took the client's chair before I could pull it back from the desk for her.

"How can I help you?" I asked.

"You know that a man was killed at the time of that trouble on Monday night?"

I liked the way she said "at the time of" instead of "in" that trouble. The way I saw it, watching from the rooftop, whatever happened to the fallen man probably had nothing to do with the riot.

"Sure," I said.

"Have they ID'd him yet?"

"Not that I've heard. Hispanic male, early to mid-twenties, no ID on him. Cause of death was gunshot wound, but they don't know what kind of weapon or who shot him."

"We know who had all the guns, though, don't we?" she said.

"We know who had the guns we could see," I said. "It's a little soon to lay this on the cops. What's your interest?"

She studied me, perhaps deciding whether a guy who didn't immediately buy in to her company line was worth trusting. She took a petulant breath and gave it a try.

"I think that man was looking for me," April Lennox said. "I think he was an undocumented Mexican national who had sneaked into Arizona to tell me his story. And I'm afraid that his story got him murdered."

A MAN HAD CALLED HER LAST FRIDAY, SHE TOLD ME. HE GAVE HIS name as Richard, but he had trouble pronouncing it, so she wondered about that. His accent sounded real, though. A native Spanish speaker, probably from northern Mexico, with enough English to get by, but not highly fluent in it. She had taken Spanish in college, and studied for a semester in Guadalajara, so she knew. The caller seemed relieved that she spoke Spanish. He said he wanted to meet her and give her a big story for her newspaper.

"Your newspaper?" I asked.

"SNC is a kind of syndication service," she said. "We sell our stories and columns to various papers around the Southwest. They're mostly alternative weeklies or small-town papers. The big outfits use their own reporters. So he must have read one of my stories. I don't know which paper he saw."

"Did you ask what his story was about?"

"Oppression and murder, he told me."

"Oppression and murder?"

"That's all he would say. It didn't bother me, because SNC gets a lot of stories that way. We take calls about oppression all the time. Not too many on murder, though. People who put themselves in danger to tell the truth have to be careful."

I thought, people who want to put *others* in danger can make up cryptic stories that appeal to potential victims. And to hungry journalists.

"How did he know you'd be here on Monday night?"

She brushed the strands of hair behind her ear.

"He didn't at first," she said. "He called my office in Los Angeles. They told him that I wouldn't be there for a few days, that I was flying over to Tucson. He said that was great. He could come up to Tucson on Monday night. They gave him my cell number."

"He said, come *up* to Tucson?" I asked.

"Right," she said. "And I figured, there's not much *down* from Tucson, is there?"

"Sixty miles or so," I said. "Then Mexico."

"Exactly. So when he called me here, I agreed to meet him in one of those restaurants on Fourth Avenue. When I talked to him, I didn't know that's where all the basketball shit would hit the fan like it did. I figured, talk to the guy, then go over to the campus. Cover whatever happened, write your basic thousand words on cops beating up kids, then go home."

"So you were going to meet him before the game?"

"Yes. We agreed to meet at five o'clock, about an hour before the game got started. I waited, but he didn't show. I watched for him when the street got war zoney, but still nothing. I thought he didn't make it to town."

"If he was illegal, he might have been leery about walking onto a street with two hundred cops."

"If he was *undocumented,*" she said, "that's surely true. And I had the sense that he was undocumented. God knows he came furtively."

"Furtively," I said. I had seen that word in reports, but I couldn't remember when I last heard an actual person say it. "So, Ms. Lennox, what do you need from me?"

She sat up straighter and leaned toward the desk.

"I want you to help me identify him. If he was my informant, then I may need some help to learn what he wanted to tell me."

"Even if we identify this victim," I asked, "how do we know he was your guy?"

"We won't, at first," she said. "It's a place to start finding out."

She was earnest and sincere, and I knew from Sal that she was a press-card-carrying journalist. But that made her request even more strange.

"You're a reporter," I said. "You should be at least as good as I am at this stuff. Why do you need me?"

"Because this is your turf. You have friends on the police force. If we do wind up in Mexico, you have experience that I don't have. I know that you were on the Border Patrol. And I know you have friends down there, too."

Wonderful, I thought. Back into the belly of the beast. A place where I had been shot at more than once, and nearly murdered twice. And my contacts down there were not the kind of people I bragged about.

"The police won't give me special information on a fresh homicide case," I said. "And having been on the Border Patrol doesn't do me any good in Mexico, believe me."

"You're close to some police and media people," she said. "It was Sal Garcia who mentioned your name to me yesterday at the chief's we-didn't-do-anything-wrong news conference. I like Sal. He does that dirty old man thing in a kind of cute, nonthreatening way."

"He'll be so pleased," I said. "Look, Ms. Lennox, why don't you give this a couple of days to shake out? The police will check missing persons reports. You and I aren't the first people to guess that this guy might be a Mexican national, so they'll check down there, too. They're running his prints now, I imagine, if they haven't already. For sure, they're interviewing in the Fourth Avenue neighborhood."

"Let it take care of itself, you mean," she said in that you-lackey-of-the-ruling-class tone.

"I mean let the professionals take care of it for now," I said. "Police don't like unexplained homicides on their city streets any more than you do. If they come up empty, and I manage to finish the cases I have working, then maybe I can help. You have any money?"

"Money?" she asked.

"Well," I said, "I know that hard-hitting journalism is essential to a great nation and all that, but investigators have to charge fees. I don't work just for love."

"Your loss," April Lennox said, smiling. She reached into her big purse. She rummaged through the clutter, pulling out a couple of small notebooks and a plastic ID card that said "LAPD Press" above her photograph. Finally she came up with a checkbook.

"Let's hold off on that for a while," I said. "First we need to be sure I can do something for you."

AL AVILA'S FRIEND JACK LINDGREN DID THIRTY YEARS ON THE TPD, retired at fifty-five with a solid pension, and took a job with the university police force. When Al called him, Jack drove his cruiser over and let us through the gate at Sancet Field. The baseball team was on a California road trip. The men shared a laugh over some cop story, then Jack returned to his car and left to fight campus crime. Al and I carried our gloves out to right field, where he had played his college games. We threw to each other, slow grounders at first, then tosses like easy fly balls and one-hop singles. The old bullet wound in my hip still twanged when I bent over, but in a few minutes I loosened up and the pain receded.

"We're checking everything we can," Al said. "Mexico looks

good to us, too. His shoes and a couple of clothing items said *Hecho en México*. Doesn't guarantee he was Mexican, but it's worth a look. You know how that goes, though, Brink. It could be weeks before we hear from anyone down there."

"And even then, who knows what they'll give you?" I said.

"Right," Al said.

Al and I had worked the Border Patrol. We grew up together, best friends since we were six years old. Not long after he left the Patrol for the Tucson police, I went private.

"Fingerprints?" I asked him.

"Negative locally. Same from AFIS. Whoever he was, the guy probably never got printed in the States. So he was never arrested or applied for a sensitive job here. He never had a visa or a recent entry permit. We figured that."

Al fired a hard throw. It wasn't like college, but he still could put some sizzle on it. He stood up straight and rolled his shoulder to lose the last kinks.

"How far can TPD go with it, Al?"

"We'll give a sketch to the media this week. We'll make sure they get it in Nogales and Agua Prieta and a couple of other places where some of the border crossers wait to come in. Don't get your hopes up. Unless some family member or friend spots the picture, or we get a missing person hit on this side, that guy's gonna be a Juan Doe."

We had stopped throwing and started walking around the perimeter of the outfield, going from right field along the fence toward deep center.

"What should I do about this reporter from L.A., do you think?"

He gave me his small, enigmatic smile and said, "What do you want to do about her, *hermano?*"

"Not that," I said. "I just wonder if I'd have a prayer of helping her."

"If nothing happens through official channels in the States," Al said, "that means you'll be helping her in Mexico. You ready to go down there, irritate the SJP and the *federales,* asking questions about a dead guy?"

I didn't answer. Al knew that I was thinking about taking a bullet on the border, and almost dying on the other side. I got no help from the State Judicial Police of Sonora or Mexican federal law enforcement then, and I wouldn't now.

"If you get jammed up," he said, "how do you take care of yourself and protect that girl? You can't carry a gun into Mexico. They'll lock you up just for that. Even a big bribe might not get you out. I go try to save your sorry butt by telling them you're a solid citizen, friend of police officers everywhere, and they say, '*Gracias por su información, capitán.* Now, *adiós.*' You want to spend a year in a cell with three pervert druggies and no toilet?"

"What would the downside be?" I asked.

"Crappy Mexican food there," he said. "It's much better in Tucson. I'd stay here and tell Ms. Reporter to go get her own stories."

Al stopped at the edge of center field, where the high left field fence rose.

"There's something else," he said.

"What?"

"Dolores is coming home to visit Anna this weekend."

He got me with that one. Dolores and Al's wife Anna were sisters. Dolores and I had lived together until one of my cases almost got her killed. Right after that, she moved to New York.

"She called last night," Al said. "She's going to stay at the house. I don't know exactly where you two stand, but it seems like a poor time to trot off to Mexico with another news babe."

"Gracias por su información, capitán," I said.

"De nada," Al said. "And you're invited to dinner."

CHAPTER 3

AL AND ANNA NEVER WANTED ME TO KNOCK. THE GIRLS, ANITA AND Alicia, usually ran to the door, but they were at a sleepover down the block. Anna greeted me with a solid maternal hug and a stern look.

"I know, I should come more often," I said. "Something smells really good."

"That could be the provocative new perfume that my sweetie gave me," Anna said, "or possibly the *chile verde* on the stove."

"You're hot," I said, "but I think it's the *chile verde* that aroused me."

"It better be," said her sweetie, walking in from the back patio. Al cocked his head in that direction and said, "Why don't you go out and say hello to Dolores?"

I walked through the family room and saw her sitting at a patio table, her back to the house. Arf, the Avilas' golden retriever, was trying to climb into her lap. His whole rear end was wagging and her face glowed with the silly pleasure of it. I went outside. Dolores turned and saw me.

"Welcome home," I said.

She smiled. Her black hair was pulled straight back and tied in a ponytail, the way she always wore it when no news consultants were butting in.

"It's so nice to be here," she said. "How are you, Brink?"

"Good. It's wonderful to see you," I said.

"All the way out on the plane," Dolores said, "I kept humming 'Feels Like Home.' It sure does. Mountains and sunsets and not one skyscraper between here and Phoenix."

"We don't build up," I said. "We just sprawl."

She laughed as Arf finally wriggled onto the chair and gave her a kiss. Dolores wore old jeans and a UA sweatshirt and no makeup. She was not fastidious about a big cuddly dog.

"He's glad to see you," I said. "He missed you."

"I'm glad to see him," she said.

Arf had preempted any awkward hugging, so I pulled out a chair and took a seat opposite Dolores.

"How's the big job?" I asked.

"Big," she said. "Pretty short on satisfaction, though."

"How so?"

"It's like you said when I left," she said. "Big station, small stories. They just have fancier toys, that's all. You know what I did last Tuesday? I staked out the private jet arrival lounge at LaGuardia, waiting for some creepy rap star to fly in from L.A. Nobody special. He hadn't killed anybody or got caught with cocaine at a playground. They just wanted his picture for the celebrity segment on the eleven o'clock newscast."

"Did you get him?"

"Yes. He said, 'I got nothing to tell the media, bitch,' then offered me a ride to Manhattan and a chance to do him in the limo."

"Those guys never play Tucson," I said. "You should come back here."

"I have a contract," she said, keeping it businesslike. "If I don't make it there, I don't make it anywhere for two years."

"I wonder," I said. "David Katz told me that employment contracts are breakable sometimes if you don't compete with the company you leave."

"Well," she said, "David's never wrong, but it hardly matters. The same few companies own everything in the business now. You move, you're competing."

"Change businesses," I said.

"I don't want to wimp out," she said. "It's the number one TV market."

"New York, New York," I said. "You've got nothing to prove, Dolores. You're beautiful, you're great at your job, you work hard, you're sincere. What more could any station want?"

"Back there," she said, "everybody's beautiful. Everybody's great at their job and everybody works their butts off. And they're all sincere, or they know how to fake it."

"The glitter rubs right off," I said.

Dolores remembered the song and smiled. She and Anna and Al and I used to sing it, riding down our own Broadway Boulevard in Al's high school blue Ford convertible.

"How about you?" she asked. "How's your job?"

"A lot of stimulating insurance work for Alejandro & Katz," I said. "David has me doing several cases right now. Some security analysis for one of their corporate clients. Found a couple of kids who ran away to the bright lights of Flagstaff."

"Uh-huh," she said. "No more murder cases?"

She knew, of course.

"Maybe," I said. "An unknown man was killed near the basketball riot. A reporter from L.A. wants somebody with local knowledge to help trace the guy and find out if he was bringing a big news story."

"An unknown man from Mexico?"

"It looks that way."

She gave Arf a little pat on the rump. The dog jumped down and wandered out to the tiny lawn.

"You're going back into Mexico?" she asked, still watching Arf.

"I don't know yet," I said.

She turned and regarded me in that wistful way that smart women look at men.

"Sure you do," she said.

ANNA'S *CHILE VERDE* WAS TERRIFIC, JUST AS SPICY AS WE ALL LIKED IT. Al put away the regular tequila and broke out the old good stuff, Herradura Añejo, to honor Dolores. We laughed through dinner, firing off old Brinker and Avila and Gonzalez family jokes, never aiming too close to the heart. By ten o'clock, we were winding down.

At the door, Al promised to call me if TPD's detectives came up with anything they would share about Juan Doe. Dolores walked me outside to my car.

"This was nice," she said.

"Yes, it was," I said.

We had stood on that spot so many times, close together, waving good night to Al and Anna and the girls. Tonight we stood apart. Al and Anna had drawn the front curtains.

"I still have nightmares," Dolores said. She did not have to explain. Before she moved to New York, a crooked Border Patrol agent kidnapped her. I had been after the guy for a murder. He took her hostage for his escape to Mexico. He wanted to kill Dolores and me. Both of us thought he would do it that night.

"Don't you?" she said.

"Not nightmares," I said. "If something more had happened to you, I don't know if I could have survived it. But I think about it every day. Every morning when I wake up in the house where we lived."

"I know that feeling, too," she said.

"We walked away from that night, but it wrecked us," I said. "That's what I think about."

We stood there quietly, looking around the street as if we had not seen it before. At this hour, the Avila neighborhood seemed deserted. The only sign of life was the bluish glow of television sets from a few front windows.

"Hear the quiet," Dolores said. "I'm so used to horns honking and sirens all night, I probably won't be able to sleep."

"Spend more time out here," I said. "You could learn to live with quiet and fresh air."

"I do miss it. The center of the universe isn't all it's cracked up to be. Still, I'd have to take an eighty percent pay cut to come from New York to Tucson."

"Feels like home, though," I said.

She smiled but said, "I can't do it, Brink. I'd be frightened every day. Not just for me. For you."

I nodded.

"Well, I better go in," she said. "Good night, Brink."

MY ANSWERING MACHINE HAD TWO MESSAGES.

"I have news about our mystery man, I think," April Lennox said. "I'll come to your office at nine tomorrow morning unless I hear from you."

On the second message, a woman's voice said, "'Johnny Get Angry.'" That was all. I hit speed dial. Gabriela Corona, over in Los Angeles, picked up on the first ring.

"Joanie Sommers," I said. "Probably 1961, maybe '62."

"It was '62, actually. Very nice work," she said. "You didn't look that up online before you called?"

"I never forget anything trivial," I said. "She sang Pepsi jingles, I think. That's pretty obscure, though. I want extra points."

We had been doing this for years, naming sixties songs and challenging each other to name the artist. Neither of us was born when the tunes were popular, but we both listened to the oldies stations.

"So," she said, "I was returning your call. You're coming to L.A. and you want me to introduce you to the pagan delights of La-La Land?"

Gabi had been a newspaper reporter in Tucson before the Los Angeles paper called. We had known each other since we were kids. When she was here and covering the Border Patrol, she'd used me for a source. Occasionally she returned the favor with information that only a good reporter could find.

"Sounds exciting, Gabi, but I'm really calling to prod you for information."

"You prodding," she said. "Be still, my heart."

Neither of us could quite remember the details, but Gabi and I used to hold hands in the fifth grade. Maybe it was fourth grade. Somewhere along the line, that ended, but we were seldom out of touch for long.

"April Lennox," I said. "You know her?"

"You want to prod *her*? Oh, well. I've seen her around. Read some of her stuff in the local weekly rag. She's all right. Rich daddy, I heard, but that's not her fault."

"She was over here for a story. She wants me to help her with it."

"Oh, please," Gabriela said. "Reporter needs detective to get story. She must be a *television* reporter. Oops. Sorry, Brink." She knew Dolores.

"It's okay," I said. "I thought the same thing. I've been around a lot of newsies. This is the first time one of them would admit to needing that kind of help on a story."

"So, what, are you hot for cute little April?"

"No," I said. "She thinks I can help her in Mexico."

"She doesn't know your colorful history down there, I guess," Gabriela said. "Well, we all have different styles, but it's not something I'd do."

"I didn't think so," I said.

"Now that you mention it, though," she said, "if I had a story in Mexico and you wanted to come along, that might be fun. Hard-hitting exposé of the Mazatlán beaches and nightlife, maybe."

"This is lowlife in Nogales, I think."

"You sure know how to pick 'em, *mijo.* You really think she just wants your detecting skills, don't you?"

"That's what she says."

Gabriela sighed. "Brinker, here's what you do," she said. "Go over to the U of A mineral museum. They've got about twenty thousand specimens there. Look around. They may just have a rock dumber than you."

"I'll be seeing you, Gabi," I said.

"Yeah," she said. "In all my old familiar places, right?"

"Only in dreams," I said.

"Ah!" she said. "Too easy." But I hung up before she could say Roy Orbison.

CHAPTER 4

THE LOCAL MORNING NEWS GEEKS CHORTLED THROUGH THEIR usual breakfast menu of sycophantic interviews with unimportant guests. As I was about to turn them off and leave for the office, one said, "Coming up, we'll talk with Tucson's police chief about the fatal murder of an unknown man at the Fourth Avenue riot." He actually said "fatal murder," but the tease still hooked me. I sank into a chair and waited through the commercials.

The chief appeared in full dress uniform. His expression never changed as he spoke. He might have OD'd on Botox. More likely, he attended a class in nonpolarizing speech for modern law enforcement team leaders. In a somnolent drone, he informed the anchors that ballistic tests had now confirmed his expectation. The unknown victim was killed by a .32-caliber bullet. No police officer assigned to Fourth Avenue that night had a .32-caliber weapon.

"I personally considered it virtually impossible that a police officer would have been involved in this incident," the chief said. The corners of his mouth looked dangerously close to turning up. "But I felt it was incumbent upon me to conduct a full investigation of that matter immediately. Now that the most far-fetched theory of this incident has been examined carefully and proven inapplicable, we can continue our search for the perpetrator or perpetrators responsible."

To my astonishment, one young anchor asked, "Chief, when you say no officer had a .32-caliber weapon, you mean officially, is that right?"

"I beg your pardon?" the chief said.

"Officially no officer had a .32," the anchor said. "But it's well known that officers sometimes carry other guns. Concealed guns."

This kid must be new, I thought. He doesn't realize that he's supposed to suck up to the big shots.

"That may happen in the movies," the chief said, sounding almost susceptible to irritation. "Our officers are not authorized to carry personal weapons in that manner."

It was clever nonresponsiveness. The anchor bought it. Whether he was out of time or out of *cojones,* he let it go and thanked the chief. I tried to imagine April Lennox watching this, throwing her coffee cup at the motel TV set.

"COULD YOU BELIEVE THAT NARCOLEPTIC NAZI?" SHE FUMED AS I LED her down the hall to my office.

"He is a little sleepy, April, but I don't think 'Nazi' is fair. People were burning cars and trashing stores. Sometimes the cops have to come down hard."

"Just because your best buddy is a police captain doesn't mean you have to defend them, Brinker."

"Al had nothing to do with the riot team," I said. "He was home watching the game."

"Oh, sure," she said, plopping into my client chair. "He's a captain. What is that in Tucson, one or two ranks below chief? He was probably in on the planning and he'll probably be in on the cover-up."

"You report, I'll decide," I said.

She shot me a disapproving look, then took a deep breath and pulled a notebook from her big cluttered purse.

"My office in L.A. gets a call yesterday morning from Hermosillo," she said. Hermosillo is the capital city of Sonora, about 150 miles south of the Arizona border.

She brushed that strand of wayward blond hair behind her ear and smiled triumphantly.

"A woman said her nephew lives in Nogales. The Mexican side. He was coming to Tucson to meet me, but they haven't heard from him since Monday afternoon," she said.

"But is he the man who was killed?" I said.

"Well, gee, let's see," she said. "A guy from Mexico arranges to see me, but doesn't show. A guy from Mexico gets killed near where we were supposed to meet. The aunt of a guy from Mexico says that guy was coming here to meet me, but hasn't been heard from since the day our guy from Mexico got killed. What do you think? Any chance of a connection there?"

"Say it's our man," I said. "Why was he up here? What did he want to tell you?"

"The woman wouldn't talk on the phone. The reporter who took the message said she told him I would have to come to Hermosillo to meet her in person."

"She's scared of something," I said.

"Well, duh," April Lennox said. "I would be, too, if my nephew got murdered and I maybe know the reason."

"Are you going down there?"

"Of course I am," she said. "It could be a great story. If it's not, well, I spend a day in a pretty Mexican town."

"If it is," I said, "you could be walking into something you can't handle. Whoever killed that guy might know that he was up here for a reason. You're the reason. If you start pushing whatever this thing is, somebody might push back."

"You'll be there to cover me," she said.

I shook my head and said, "I don't think so, April."

"Don't wimp out on me, Brinker," she said. "I can do it myself, but I'd feel better with a sidekick on this one."

"If you insist on going, stay out in the open," I said. "Fly in, meet the woman in some public place. Buy her lunch at the Plaza Zaragosa. Fly back to the States on the same day. Sort out the information at home, kick it around with your editors, and decide what to do."

"I don't believe this," she said. She stood up, ran her hand forcefully through the errant blond hair, and put her hands on her hips. "I heard that you had some balls. Bad information, huh?"

"April, not doing it your way isn't necessarily a failure of courage. The lawyers here sign my checks. They're my friends, too. I was jammed up with a grand jury last year and David Katz made the whole thing go away. He wouldn't take a dime. So they get first claim on my time, and they have cases waiting for me right now."

"Oh, fine," she said. "Making the world safe for some predatory insurance company, I suppose."

I had to laugh. "Yep, that's my life's work."

"Uh-huh," she said. "Well, go for it, then." She slung the big purse over her shoulder and started for the door. She turned back and said, "You can read about it when I crack this thing."

"April," I said, "you're not going for a weekend at Acapulco or a trek to Chichén Itzá. I know you speak the language, but it's another world down there. You may be messing with people who've already risked a murder in the States. They won't think twice about another one in Mexico."

"Oh, for chrissakes," she said. "I'll be sipping tea with some lady at a sidewalk café on a plaza in the middle of the day. How dangerous can that be?"

"Watch yourself," I said.

"I guess I'll have to," she said. "Nobody else will."

CHAPTER 5

BUTCH AND SUNDANCE HAD JUST BLOWN THE DOOR OFF THE RAILroad car. Money was floating down around them. How many real crooks look as good as those guys? I wondered. Hector Ortiz, the young drug lord of Nogales, Sonora, maybe. I had not seen Hector since he saved Dolores's life and mine. If I never went back to Mexico, I probably would never see him again.

It was another big evening at the Brinker house, watching old movies on cable and supporting the NAFTA countries' beer industries. Depression was about to set in when the phone rang.

"Brinker," April Lennox said. I was surprised to realize that I recognized her voice. She said, "If I have to sit around the motel for another night, I'll go crazy. Crazier. What are you doing?"

"Sitting around the house for another night," I said.

"Well, then," she said. "Look, I was kind of a jerk today. Peace offering?"

"Okay."

"I just happen to have a nice California cabernet tucked in a brown paper bag here. I'll bet you have a couple of glasses."

I laughed and said, "How long till you get here?"

"Give me thirty seconds," she said. "I'm parked by your mailbox."

I heard her car tires crunch along the gravel driveway. By the time I got to my front door, she was standing there. She wore her usual khaki slacks with a forest-green sweater. The bulky purse hung from her shoulder. She held out a brown paper bag.

"McManis," she said. "Yummy but not famous yet. Next year, the word will be out and I won't be able to afford it."

We walked through the entryway and into the living room. She stopped to survey the place, looking a bit like a reporter getting local color for a feature story.

"I was expecting one of those desiccated cow skulls on the wall," she said. "A Remington print, maybe."

"You should check into a dude ranch," I said. "They have all that stuff for you tourists. Chuckwagon dinners with cowboy steak and baked beans. Songs around the campfire."

"Just like *Blazing Saddles,*" she said. "Disgusting. I'll stick with the motel. Open the wine, will you?"

I got two balloon glasses and a corkscrew from the kitchen and brought them back to the heavy Mexican wood table in the living room.

"You were expecting juice glasses from Wal-Mart, right?" I said.

She flopped down on the worn leather couch. It had been in my grandparents' house since long before I was born. They gave it to my parents when they moved to a small condo, not long before they died. My parents gave it to me.

"Okay," April said. "I'm a snob. I'll stop. Just pour the wine."

"We shouldn't let it breathe?" I said.

"Oh, cut it out," she said. She smiled, though. "I stopped, already."

We clinked and drank. I sipped mine, but April took a deep, workday-is-done pull of hers.

"Yummy is right," I said.

She smiled and said, "Told you. I could give you the whole oenophile routine, but you'd start feeling inferior."

I shrugged and rolled the rich red wine around in the big glass. Streaks of cabernet drifted in creamy rivulets to the bottom. April was stretching out on the sofa.

"Nice legs," I said.

"Thanks," she said.

"The wine," I said.

"I know what you meant," she said.

The television flickered at the other side of the room. Butch and Sundance were riding in the mountains of Colombia or Bolivia or wherever they went to play out the western bandit string. April ran her hand along the armrest at the end of the old sofa. It was worn there, more beige than brown.

"Lot of heads rested here," she said. She kept moving her fingertips around on the leather.

"Three generations that I know of," I said. "My dad had thick hair, but he wore it cut really short. When I was a little guy, I'd stand at the end of the couch while he was lying there. I'd rub his hair with my hand. It felt like a wire brush. At least it felt that way to a kid. Maybe that's what wore it down."

April turned away as if to study the leather's grain.

"Haven't thought of that for years," I said. "Saying it now, I can actually feel it on the palm of my hand."

April looked up and seemed to gather herself. There was that tiny damp sparkle at the edge of her eye, but her voice was clear and warm.

"It's a nice memory to have," she said. She took the wine bottle from the table and half filled her glass.

"How did you know where I live?" I asked.

"I don't have to reveal my sources," she said. "Are you angry?"

"Only if bad guys follow me home," I said.

"I hope I don't qualify on either count."

"No."

She sat up and crossed her legs under her butt in a way that only young women and yoga masters seem able to manage. She held the bowl of the wineglass in both hands.

"But you think I'm an idiot, don't you?"

"Why would you say that, April?" I thought she smiled a bit when I spoke her name.

"Because," she said, "at your office, you act like I'm some kind of smartass sophomoric lefty agitator kid who doesn't know when she's in over her head." She did not seem angry as she said these things. She seemed curious.

"I don't think that, April," I said. "But look. Lots of people *do* get in over their heads when they poke around in Mexico. I did. It almost got me killed."

"You and Miss Gonzalez," she said.

I nodded. April drank more wine. She put the glass down and pushed the lock of blond hair behind her ear.

"What about her?" she said.

I shook my head and looked out the window, into the desert night. Just enough moonlight shone to cast my two saguaros and my neighbor's eucalyptus trees in silhouette.

"I don't know," I said. "She doesn't know. We've been apart a long time."

"How come that's always so hard to know?" she said. "You'd think that would be one thing that's easy to feel certain about."

"You'd think," I said. "Was it ever, for you?"

Now it was April's turn to look away. She watched the silent television. Butch and Sundance were hunkered down in the bank, nearing their freeze frame in outlaw lore. She looked at pictures on the table beside me, Al and Anna, the girls, Dolores and me, at the Desert Museum.

She leaned far across the edge of the table and took my hand.

"Come over here," she said. She pulled gently on my hand and I found myself moving toward the sofa. She moved over and guided me into the place at the end.

"April," I said, but she quieted me by putting her finger softly to my lips.

"I'm not hitting on you," she said. "I get it about your not knowing. But I just can't go be alone in that godforsaken motel room for another night. Okay?"

"Okay," I said.

She turned herself around, lying across my lap with her head on the sofa's armrest.

"Just stay here a little while," she said.

Sometime before midnight, I wriggled out from under her. She barely stirred. I brought a pillow and a blanket from the guest room. When I lifted her head to put the pillow under it, her eyes opened slightly. She whispered something that might have been, "Thank you."

I fell into the chair opposite her and dozed. In the small hours, something woke me. Faint desert moonlight dusted the ceiling. April seemed to be sobbing quietly, her face turned away from me. I moved closer and saw tears on her cheek. When I touched her arm and spoke to her, she did not respond. Her crying stopped in time. I drifted back to sleep. As morning's light began to fill the room, I awoke again to see her hand clinging to the worn spot on the armrest.

We said nothing about the night as we made orange juice and coffee and toast. We moved silently, gingerly about the kitchen in an uneasy ballet, as if we had been one-night lovers. She used the shower and gathered her things. I walked her to the door. She stood on her tiptoes and kissed me on the mouth and said, "If she's still your girlfriend, you can tell her that you were good. And kind. I like you, Brinker."

And before I could say a thing, she put a single finger to my lips as she had the night before. She said, "Tell me no lies," then turned and walked purposefully to her car.

Before she opened the car door, she said, "I'll call you tomorrow. Maybe talk you into going to Mexico. Think about it, at least?"

"Okay," I said.

CHAPTER 6

I DECIDED TO CALL APRIL. ONE MORE TRY TO TALK HER OUT OF MEXico. But if she remained determined to go, I would go with her. Get in, interview her mystery woman, get out.

Then David Katz tapped on my open office door and walked in.

"We should buy lottery tickets," he said. "It's our lucky day, my boy."

I looked up from typing an insurance interview report. "How's that?" I asked.

"A lead on Will Norman's daughter," he said. He handed me a small piece of notepaper with a telephone number written in red ink. The area code was 480.

"She called him," David said.

Will Norman was a real estate developer whose name was on half the subdivisions in greater Tucson. Like all developers here, he had his share of fans and sworn enemies. Some people thought he made Arizona living affordable for the working class. Others said he raped the land to clutter it with ticky-tacky.

"Don't tell me she left a number," I said. Danielle Norman, seventeen years old, had been missing for almost four months. She drove to Scottsdale for Christmas shopping and never came back. Her car was found in the shopping center parking lot.

"Caller ID," David said.

"You're kidding," I said.

"Stranger things have happened," David said. He leaned over and pushed the number closer to me. "Priority one, Brink."

He did not need to say why. Norman was a client and a long-time close friend. David Katz was not a demonstrative man, but I saw him embrace Will Norman, the two of them in tears. Norman was a widower and David thought losing Danielle might kill him. David offered the services of the firm, day and night, to help find his daughter. I spent most of a month on it. Like many of the runaways and the stolen children, though, she seemed to have fallen off the planet. Eventually, David told me to keep my eyes open, but move on.

"Don't let Will get his hopes up," I said. "It could be a pay phone, or a stolen cell phone, or a computer-spoofed number. The area code says east valley, but with technology these days, she could be in New Jersey or New Delhi."

"Let's find out," David said.

"What did she say?"

"Just that she knew he would be worried. She said she's okay. He should not try to find her. Will said she didn't sound okay."

"If she's being held, David, this fits a pattern. The kidnapper thinks he has her softened up, on his side."

"Stockholm syndrome," David said.

"Something like that," I said. "He tells her to call. She goes along because the kidnapper promises her something if she does."

"Or," David says, "threatens to withhold something if she doesn't."

"Right. Hearing her father's voice might have snapped her out of it, though. Parents, house, friends."

"Why would he have her call?"

"I've seen this before," I said. "The kidnapper believes he can take the heat off if the victim seems to be okay. It doesn't work that way, but these guys don't think it out."

"Can you imagine what she's been through?" he said.

"I don't have to imagine. I've seen it, for real."

"Get on this now, please," David said. He turned and walked toward his office, head down, pulling a handkerchief from his pocket.

I CALLED QWEST. THE OPERATOR CONFIRMED THAT IT WAS ONE OF THEIR numbers, somewhere in the east valley suburbs of Phoenix. She would not say what city, or whether the phone was residential or business or pay phone. That was fine. My first fear had been a cell phone with a bogus address, but now I had ruled that out.

Tracing the number was trickier. I could get Al to run it. Will Norman had filed a missing persons report with TPD, after all. I could call in a favor from my friend at the Arizona Corporation

Commission. He worked on telco regulation. Getting a number would be no problem for him.

Keep it simple, Brinker. I decided to try a reverse directory on the Internet first. It's a public page. Anybody can type in a phone number. If the number is listed, the site provides a name and address. Sure enough, the information splashed onto my computer screen: R. Alexander, a Paradise Valley address.

Let this be as easy as it looks, I thought. Let R. Alexander be as dumb as he seems.

INTERSTATE 10 WAS WIDE OPEN. I SAILED ALONG IN THE SLIPSTREAM of an eighteen-wheeler and got to Scottsdale in ninety minutes, my personal best. I gassed up and bought a newspaper at a convenience store. Time enough to call April when I found the address and checked out the situation there.

Paradise Valley is mostly north of Camelback Road and west of Scottsdale Road. I found the address in one of the modest old residential neighborhoods not yet bladed for overpriced condos. That fit. You couldn't easily hold an unwilling teenager in an apartment building. But the R. Alexander place, a 1950s bungalow on its own untended half-acre, looked perfect.

A few residents or visitors parked their cars on the street. I drove south, about half a block past Alexander's place, and pulled to the curb. My rearview mirrors were angled to give me good looks at the house and yard. The bungalow had an attached garage, not just the carport usually found in old, cheap desert homes. The door was down. Handy if you want to minimize sights of your comings and goings, I thought. I could see two windows from my position. One was the front room, facing the street. The other probably was a bedroom and the south end of the house. Curtains were drawn at both.

At 12:15, I heard the garage door open. A seventies-vintage Chrysler Cordoba backed out. The once-burgundy paint had been dulled by decades of Arizona sun. The rich Corinthian leather looked cracked and torn even from a block away. The driver was an Anglo man, fortyish, with a thin neck, narrow shoulders, a pale complexion and short dark hair. He sat forward, close to the steering wheel, so I made him for short height. I saw him raise a remote control device to the car window. The garage door started down.

Decision time. If this was R. Alexander, and if he was going to work for eight hours, I had to think about going in. But 12:15 seemed like the wrong time to head for a job. What shift would that be? I decided to stay put.

Good move. At 12:33, the Cordoba eased back down the street. The door started up before the car reached the driveway. Once inside the garage, the man stepped from the car and looked casually up and down the block. He did not seem to pay any attention to my car. He carried two bags from a fast-food burger chain. He stepped up to the house door and hit a button on the frame. The garage door came down again.

I kept a list of phone numbers in a small notebook in my glove compartment. The number for Paradise Valley's police department was there. I used my cell phone and asked for a detective named Cliff Billings.

"Brinker," he said. "How may we be of service today?"

Billings had helped me on a runaway case the year before. He struck me as a good cop who liked to get the job done quickly, without a lot of police bureaucracy.

"Jimmy Hoffa's buried under Lincoln Drive," I said.

"Good," he said. "I'll stop traffic and dig the place up right away."

"I think I've got a Tucson girl, age seventeen, likely kidnap, in a house on your turf," I said.

"You *think*?"

"She called her father. He had caller ID, and the number came back to this house."

"Nobody's that stupid," Billings said.

"Want to bet?"

"No," he said. "You're there?"

"Yes," I said. I told him where the house was and gave him R. Alexander's name and phone.

"Hmm," he said. I heard him tapping at a keyboard, then silence, then a few more taps.

"Solid citizen," he said. "No warrants, no wants, no calls to the house for anything."

"Yet," I said.

"Too bad he's not a terrorist," he said. "We could just crash in there, ship him to Gitmo. End of story."

"I've been doing this a long time, Billings. She's in there."

"I've been doing this a while, too, Brinker, and I know what makes a judge sign a search warrant for a local taxpayer's house. A phone call tip from an out-of-town PI ain't it. No disrespect."

"None taken," I said. "What if I personally see this girl and call you?"

"Then I'll be there with the red-and-blues flashing. Do I need to remind you of Arizona Revised Statute Section 13-1502?"

"Criminal trespass," I said. "I learned all about that at private investigator school."

"I don't know about Tucson, but we actually enforce that one in this jurisdiction," Billings said. "Call me if you're right. If you're wrong, I'll book your ass."

"Fair enough," I said.

AT 3:35, I WAS JUST ABOUT TO CALL APRIL WHEN THE PARADISE Valley taxpayer opened his garage door and surveyed the street again. Now he was wearing fresh khaki slacks and a blue golf shirt with the logo of a big box home improvement store. When he turned around, I saw a larger store logo on his back. He must work there. Four-to-midnight shift? Did those places stay open that late? I flipped through my newspaper and found the ad. "Spring Super Sale," it said. "All stores open 'til midnight tonight and tomorrow." Bingo. By the time I looked up, R. Alexander was driving away.

I scanned the block. No streetlights on either side. Going in at night would give me a big edge, but it was three and a half hours until sunset. If I could be sure that he would stay gone . . .

The newspaper ad gave six addresses for branches of the home improvement store. Two were nearby. I got lucky at the first one, on Cactus Road near the Scottsdale airport. The Cordoba sat there, courteously parked in a far corner of the lot so customers could use the close-in spaces. He was here, all right, and surely working late.

The store shared its parking lot with a cluster of fast-food places. I used the rest room at one, then bought a sandwich and soda. I sat at a table by the window, keeping an eye on R. Alexander's car. The home improvement store stayed busy. People were getting off work now, stopping to shop before heading home.

Three teenage girls came into the restaurant, ordered, and brought salads to a table near mine. They were laughing in that utterly carefree way of the young, enjoying every moment with each other. I wondered if Danielle Norman had been that way with her friends in the days before she vanished.

Was she in Alexander's house now? God knows he could have her tied up in a shack out in the desert somewhere. But I was betting on the bungalow. I headed back there as the shadows lengthened, then softened, and the blue springtime sky gave way to gray.

HE WOULD NOT HAVE A BURGLAR ALARM. I HAD HANDLED A CASE like this before. The weirdo who held a teenage girl hostage in his house near Tubac astonished me by saying that he had no security system. But it made sense when I thought about it.

"You don't want an alarm blaring," the kidnapper told me. "The cops would come if neighbors complained about the noise. If you have a silent alarm, police usually won't even show up. But it might be a slow night. They might have a car close by. I'd rather take my chances."

So I took mine. I grabbed the short tire jack handle from my car trunk, tucked it and my gun into my jacket, checked the block for traffic, and strolled onto R. Alexander's lot. I rang the front doorbell. No answer. I turned around, looking ready to leave, and saw no one watching from other houses. My guess was that R. Alexander had few fast friends among his neighbors, nobody watching out for his place. I walked casually around the garage to the back.

The back door was a glass slider with a second track of burglar bars. The bars wouldn't budge. I tried bending them with the jack handle. They held solid. He had a cheap-looking house, but he bought good accessories when he needed them. The only other rear access was a kitchen window, but it had the iron bars, too.

I walked around the other end of the house. Another barred window. But this one looked different when I came close. There was no sense of space behind the curtains. Some kind of interior wall had been built or placed against the curtains. If I was right, it was there to block noise and thwart an escape.

Danielle Norman was in there. I could not get to her from the back of the house. I stood there, frustrated and angry. These guys always screw up somewhere, I thought, just like R. Alexander did with the caller ID. Where had he messed up here?

I returned to the front and found the big window there barred, too. That left the door. He'll have it reinforced, I figured. Maybe a metal frame or even a second door behind the visible one. I shoved the jack handle's pointed end into the space between the door and the frame. I put my weight behind the handle. The wood was soft, and the spot around the lock plate gave way. There's his mistake, I thought. He must have believed that nobody breaks in through a front door. Maybe he'll meet some burglars in prison who can straighten him out about that.

I worked the handle in deeper. The edge of the door moved. I levered the jack handle against the iron latch, pressed my shoulder against the wood, and shoved until the frame gave way and the door fell open. I hurtled into the front room, stumbled, and fell on the floor. I rolled over and kicked the door shut. It wouldn't close all the way, but it might not be noticed from the street.

The whole thing, from the time I shoved the jack handle into the door, took about fifteen seconds. If anybody saw me, I probably had three to five minutes before the cops arrived. I headed to my left, toward a short narrow hallway. The door on the left would lead to the room where I thought the window was blocked off. I took out my gun, turned the doorknob, and pushed gently. The door was heavy, not the cheesy wood frame I expected to find. As it opened, I could see that the wall and the door itself were covered with a foot of padding. I looked up and saw that more padding, like a quilt of mattresses, had been installed beneath the ceiling.

When I pushed the door fully open, I saw that room contained a cell, a free-standing, covered cubicle of black iron bars. It was about eight feet square and maybe six feet high. The only object inside was a foam pad, and sitting on it, huddled in the corner, wearing a drab blue bathrobe, watching me with fearful eyes, was Danielle Norman. She was gaunt and her face was pale from confinement and months of unbroken misery.

"Danielle," I said. "I'm from Tucson, and I'm going to get you home."

She said, in such a deadened voice that I strained to hear, "He'll kill you. He'll kill me."

"No chance, Danielle," I said. "He's finished." Her expression did not change.

I walked to the cage door. It had a steel lock built into the frame and the door. I couldn't get in without a key or an acetylene torch.

"Do you know where he keeps the key?" I asked.

"No," she said. "It's on his key ring. After he unlocks the door, he puts it in his pocket."

"I'm calling the cops now," I said. "They'll have the equipment to get you out."

She did not respond. But when I started for the room door, she said, "Don't leave."

"I'm just going to the phone, Danielle. Next room. I'll be right back." She looked at me doubtfully.

R. Alexander had an old rotary phone. No wonder he didn't know about caller ID. I called the Paradise Valley police and asked for Billings. Against all odds, he was still there.

"I've got her," I said.

"No shit? Where, at the house?"

"Yeah. You'll need bolt cutters or maybe a torch to get her loose. Bring a female officer, sexual offenses detail, if you have one. I'll open the front door, but I've gotta stay with her. Tell your guys I'm keeping my gun, but I'll have my hands up and empty when I hear them come in."

"Okay," Billings said. "This isn't going to screw up my career, is it?"

"Yeah," I said. "They'll make you chief."

BILLINGS AND SIX UNIFORMS GOT THERE IN FOUR MINUTES. THE patrolmen patted me down and took my gun. I told Billings where to find R. Alexander and his car. In another five minutes, a female in tailored jeans, running shoes, and a bulky white sweater walked in. She nodded at Billings and went straight to the corner of the cage where Danielle Norman still cringed. The woman pulled the sweater above her belt to show Danielle the badge fastened there. She reached through the bars and took the girl's hand. For the first time, Danielle moved, edging herself closer to the bars. The woman spoke quietly to her for a moment, then caught Billings's eye and nodded to the door.

"Let's us guys take it outside," Billings said. When the uniforms moved to grab my arms, the detective said, "He's all right."

We walked out to the police cars, three marked units with the lights flashing and a dark blue sedan. Billings leaned against his unmarked unit and lit a cigarette.

"I need to reach her father," I said.

He tossed me his cell phone. I called David Katz and told him. He said he would contact Will Norman.

"They'll probably take her to a hospital tonight," I said. "Detective Billings can give you directions."

Billings took the phone and spoke with Katz for a few moments. When he hung up, he stared at the bungalow.

"Just when you think you've seen everything," he said.

"Yeah."

"I've got a twelve-year-old daughter."

I nodded, but couldn't say anything to make that thought any less frightening.

Billings said, "Missing girls, you know, half the time they just ran off with some greasy-haired guitar player. Or they're hitchhiking to Maine to get out of the heat and piss off their parents. This here, this is truly weird shit. That girl's lucky we found her now."

A panel truck pulled up to the curb. A welding supply company name and address was painted on the side doors. A woman in dark blue work pants and an ASU sweatshirt got out. She loaded an air tank and some other supplies onto a dolly, tucked a welder's helmet under her arm, and walked toward the house. She said, "Hi, Cliff."

"Thanks for coming so fast, Ronnie," Billings said.

Next came the ambulance. One of the paramedics laughed and said something about the Diamondbacks. Billings just jerked his head toward the door. The paramedics got the message and hurried inside.

We heard hissing and clanking and banging and, finally, the loud thunk of something big and metallic hitting the floor. Not a minute later, the paramedics came out with Danielle on a stretcher. The female cop still held her hand, walking along beside. They put the stretcher into the ambulance.

The female cop walked back to Billings. "I'm going with her," she said. "He didn't attack her today, for a change, so I don't know what we'll get for physical evidence. She's pretty bewildered right now. Post-trauma. But she seems like a tough kid. She can probably do a lineup tomorrow or the next day."

"She tell you much?" Billings asked.

"Enough to put that creep away forever," the woman said. "If I don't fillet him first."

BILLINGS TOOK MY STATEMENT AT THE COP SHOP, THEN RETURNED my gun and cut me loose. A uniform drove me back to the bungalow. Crime scene techs were still there. A neighborhood crowd had gathered. The TV crews were wrapping up after their late news live shots. I didn't need to see the interviews: "We're shocked. He was such a quiet man. . . ."

When I reached I-10, fatigue hit me like a sledgehammer. No way I could drive for almost two hours without running off the road. I saw a sign for a cheap motel at the Baseline exit. I fell onto the bed, fully dressed, and knew nothing else until rush-hour traffic shook me awake the next morning.

I remembered a Starbucks in the Arizona Mills center across the street. I drove over there, got a double tall latte and a bottle of orange juice, and checked my messages at home. David Katz had called to say that he and Will Norman had reached the hospital. His voice broke when he described the father-daughter reunion.

"Will has a bonus for you," David said. "You really did hit the lottery, Brink."

The next message was from April Lennox. She had left it the morning before.

"Hi," she said. "I tried to call you at the office. I left some messages, but, well, I guess you have something going on. Look, I have to go to Mexico now. I found out something, um, something new. The story's looking even more important. To me, I mean. So I'm going to leave right now. I'll call you when I get back."

The next message, too, was from April. "Hi, again. Um, I just wanted to say thanks for the other night. You were nice. I wish you could come with me, but, well, like I said, your loss. 'Bye."

There was a pause, maybe ten seconds, then she hung up.

APRIL LENNOX LEFT, BUT THE BEAUTIES OF HER NAMESAKE MONTH remained. The sun rose sooner, bringing a hint of warmth to the desert's fresh morning air. The prickly pear cactus blossoms began to burst open, short-lived and delicate flowers on those tough spiny plants, rich reds and yellows dotting their dusty green skins.

I heard nothing from April. I left messages on her cell number. I called Southwest News Consortium in L.A. They didn't know where she was. They didn't seem worried. That's the way she works, a reporter told me.

Al and Anna and the girls asked me to Easter dinner. Anna served roast lamb with a sweet ruby jelly that she made from the prickly pear in their own yard. We ate out there at the big wooden table. Alicia sitting on my left, Anita on my right. They chattered and teased and competed for my attention. The sky was such a bright, unbroken blue that we needed sunglasses.

Just after dinner, Dolores called from New York and got the girls laughing. She said she was glad to hear my voice, too. Anna took the phone and moved away to speak softly. I could not hear her, but once or twice she dabbed at her eyes with a handkerchief. It was a holiday, a true holy day for her, and she wanted her sister at the family table.

Something Dolores said made Anna look at me. Her eyes still glistened. She turned away and continued the conversation. I had no idea what Dolores wanted. I didn't know where April Lennox was. But I had perhaps saved a young girl's life. I had put a very bad man out of business. My bank balance was in the black and would be for a long while. I had just spent a perfect Sunday in the company of my life's greatest friends. The soft evening seemed filled with spring's promise.

Often, I am wrong.

CHAPTER 7

On Tuesday of the last week in April, Tommy O'Mara called me. He was a TPD homicide detective, a big graying redhead with a don't-bullshit-a-bullshitter attitude and few social graces. Some people found him hard to take, but he was a thorough, conscientious cop. Al said to me once, "Tommy thinks I'm just a dumb affirmative action Mexican. But if I ever get put down, I hope Tommy draws the case."

"What's up, O'Mara?" I said.

"Just got off the horn from the U.S. Consulate in Nogales," he said. "Guy named Miguel Calderón. You ever run into him?"

"I don't think so," I said.

"After your time on the border, maybe. Anyway, he got a call from SJP on a homicide down there. They're pretty sure it's an American citizen. On the edge of town, near the *maquiladoras*."

What are the State Judicial Police of Sonora investigating that involves me? I thought.

"The woman didn't have a purse or the usual ID or anything. But the clothes and the haircut and the dental work, the Mexicans think she's from our side. So this guy Calderón is checking to see if we have any missing persons who fit the description. And he wondered if I knew you."

"How come?" I asked, not wanting to hear the answer. I think I had known when he said, "the woman."

"Only identifying thing she had on her was your business card. It was tucked into a little inside pocket flap in her slacks. Kind of thing a robber in a hurry could have missed."

"Aw, Jesus," I said.

"Tell me," O'Mara said.

"I hope I'm wrong," I said. "Late twenties, short blond hair, blue eyes?"

"Uh-oh," he said. "I'm sorry, man."

"She had an L.A. press card," I said. "LAPD or county sheriff, I don't remember. Either way, her prints will be on file over there. Have the Mexican cops send their victim's prints to L.A. and they'll get a match on April Lennox. The Secret Service might even have them if she covered any presidential visits." I spelled her last name for him and told him where she had worked.

"They already took the prints," O'Mara said. "This'll speed things up. Look, it's not my jurisdiction, but I'd like to help the Mexicans and our consulate on this one. Might need them someday. You better come down here and tell me what the hell happened."

AT HIS OFFICE, WHEN I ASKED HIM, HE SAID, "YOU REALLY WANT TO know?"

"I need to know," I said.

"Raped and manual strangulation," O'Mara said. "They don't know which was first, but that'll come out in the autopsy. Her clothes had been ripped off, left in a pile beside her body. There's not much sign of struggle. No hand bruises or skin under her fingernails."

"Something's wrong there," I said.

"That's what I'm thinking. I told Calderón and he said he'd tell the Mexican cops. I wish we could get her body back to the States. Get some relative to pay for an autopsy here."

"Gabi Corona told me that April's father is wealthy. He'd do that."

"You have a contact for him?" O'Mara asked.

"I don't, but they probably will at her job."

He made a note. "Okay," he said. "So, what happened with this woman, Brinker?"

I told him what little I knew. The riot, the dead man on the side street, April's visit, the mystery man's call, her decision to go alone to Mexico just before I would have joined her.

"The Juan Doe, I knew about him," O'Mara said. "Not my case. It started in internal affairs because of the riot. Once they figured no cop did it, IA kicked it to Puente. But any homicide here, we all keep an eye out. Three weeks now, and that guy's still in the fridge. We don't know who he is. If there was an aunt in

Hermosillo or wherever, how come nobody's claimed him?"

"If April never connected with the aunt, the family may not know he's dead," I said. "If she did meet the aunt and told her what happened, maybe the family is afraid of something."

"Lotta guesswork here," O'Mara said. "We don't even know if she got to Hermosillo."

"I let that girl down," I said.

"Way too hard on yourself," O'Mara said.

"I should have gone with her. I was going to, but I didn't call her in time."

"What, there's some law that says you have to take any case that walks in the door? She was a rabble-rousing reporter. It's a dangerous calling. She went into a place where press cards and the Bill of Rights don't mean squat. And if it was some psycho perv that got her, hell, that could happen here."

"It's not like she was just getting stonewalled on information," I said. "What is there about this thing, asking questions about Juan Doe, that got her murdered?"

O'Mara leaned back in his chair. He rolled his shoulders and massaged his neck. "Might not have been that," he said.

"What, a mugging? You're kidding."

"Not that," he said. "But there's some strange things happening down there. Last two years, there've been about ten women murdered in Nogales. Bodies found not far from your girl. Sex angles, like on this one. A few of them were prostitutes, so that might have happened in the normal course of rough trade in a border town. But they were all locals. No Americans."

"Two years?" I said. "I haven't heard anything about this."

"Brown-skinned people in a third world country," O'Mara

said. "Doesn't get a lot of play in the local media. Not a real advertiser-friendly story."

"Serial killer? Come on, O'Mara. The press loves that stuff."

"Yeah, well, I'm just saying. You remember that pretty little blond girl, got kidnapped by some religious wacko in Utah? The press went absolutely ballistic. We could have had nuclear war and they wouldn't have backed off that kidnap story. Well, there was a little black girl kidnapped about the same time. Similar case, you know? She just vanished from her house. She didn't get diddly on national TV."

O'Mara wasn't known for his sensitivity or tolerance. I was surprised to hear him talk this way.

"I didn't know them," I said, "but I knew April Lennox. I let her down."

"I'm just saying," O'Mara went on, as if I hadn't spoken, "these women in Nogales. They were hookers and poor housewives and factory workers. Probably lived in those cardboard houses on the side of a hill. Nobody gives a shit."

"You do," I said.

"We gotta try to solve them all," O'Mara said. "But this isn't my case. It's not even my country. I dunno, maybe this April Lennox thing will get some attention. Another pretty blond girl."

We sat there for a few moments, looking around the walls of O'Mara's office.

"What can you do with this?" I asked.

"Nada," he said. "It happened in Mexico. The only way TPD would get into it, there'd have to be a connection between the Juan Doe murder and her. I'll pitch it, Brinker, but the lieutenant's

not gonna think it's enough to pull our guys off their own cases. Even then, we'd still need cooperation from the Mexicans."

"Yeah, right," I said.

"Exactly," O'Mara said. "Lots of fuckin' luck. I'm sorry, man, but for now, I can't go anywhere with this."

"I can," I said.

CHAPTER 8

HOLLYWOOD PARK RACETRACK APPEARED IN MY WINDOW WHEN THE Southwest jet popped through morning coastal scud. We squealed onto the LAX runway a minute later. I drove my rental car up the 405, east on the Santa Monica to Fairfax, and headed north.

The route felt familiar. Over the years, I traced a dozen runaway kids from Tucson to Los Angeles. Many of them had wound up in the downscale sections of the west side. They dreamed of Beverly Hills or Malibu, but made it only as far as cheap apartments in Hollywood and Little Ethiopia, often at the mercy of someone little better than R. Alexander.

Southwest News Consortium operated from a nondescript strip mall on Melrose, well east of the trendy restaurants and *très cher* shops. Its offices in the brown block building sat between a tattoo parlor and a smoking supplies store. The front door opened directly to a small newsroom. A few people worked at computer terminals or took notes as they spoke on telephones. Others stood around, holding coffee cups and chatting.

I must have thought that everyone would look like April Lennox. The crowd was older than I expected, and the place seemed time-warped. Posters of Jimi and Janis and Boss Radio 93 KHJ hung on the walls. I should tell Gabi Corona about this place, I thought.

"Hi, there," said the stout lady with long gray hair who sat at the first desk. Mama Cass, had she lived, I thought. She wore a flowery muumuu, a telephone headset, and a blissful smile. She had a pen in hand, poised over a book of phone message slips. "Help you?"

I gave her my card and told her that I had an appointment with Ralph Jameson.

"You're Brinker, then," she said, looking more serious. "Back there, in the office on the right." She pointed to a glass-enclosed area at the rear of the newsroom. I could see a slender man with short gray hair, staring intently at his computer monitor.

"Don't worry," the receptionist said. "He's just playing Free Cell. It takes him a while to get started in the morning."

"Watch it," I said. "You'll get fired."

"Not as long as I tuck him in at night," she said.

Jameson stood as I knocked on his open door. We shook hands and made our introductions. He pointed me to a chair and sank into his own, behind the desk.

"Awful thing," he said. He looked awful himself, with baggy eyes, a couple of days' stubble, and a cheap white shirt that had not been near a laundry lately. "You know what the worst part of it is?"

"What?"

"You're the first person who's shown any real interest in this," he said. "I had one call from a Tucson cop. We've heard nothing from the Mexican police. We sent a reporter down there, of course. Good man, solid reporter. He was born in Mexico. Speaks perfect Spanish. But even he can't break through. Nobody knows anything. I'm going to have to pull him out tomorrow. We're not made of money."

"What about her father?" I asked. "Can't he buy some investigation?"

He looked at me, puzzled. "Old man Lennox didn't hire you?" he said.

"No."

"When you called, I just assumed the father had hired private help. No action from official agencies, so he decided to take things into his own hands."

"I'll try to see him while I'm here," I said. "But I have never spoken to him."

"So," Jameson said, "who did hire you?"

"Nobody," I said. "April tried to, but I turned her down."

"Ah," he said. "You're doing penance." When I didn't answer, he said, "Well, whatever you're doing, we'll help all we can. What do you need?"

"She was going to contact a woman in Hermosillo who had called this office. Somebody took a message and relayed it to April."

Jameson nodded. "That was Jon Cartwright. He was working at April's desk while she was in Tucson. He wrote down the name and number. When April called, he gave the information to her, then tossed it. No way he could remember. He did recall the woman's name. It was Esposito, but that hardly narrows it down in Mexico. Or here, for that matter."

He closed his eyes and put his hands to his temples like a man with a migraine. "Jesus, we're supposed to be in the information business. We let the most important bit of information get away."

"I'd like to talk to Cartwright," I said.

"He's on vacation in Colorado. Up in some canyon beyond the range of cell phones, he says. He's kind of shaken by all this. They were close once, Jon and April. He had to get away. He'll be home in a couple of days, though. I'll give him your number."

He tapped his fingers on the desktop and stared out toward the newsroom.

"April was kind of a loner on stories," he said. "I let her do it her way, because that's how we play it here, and because she always delivered the goods. She was here three years and I don't think we ever had to run a correction on her stuff. Got complaints from idiots who can't handle the truth, but that's fine. Her information was always solid."

He paused and shook his head. "But you know, if she had been a little more collaborative, or if I had kept her on a little tighter leash . . ."

"She was independent," I said. "I could see that the minute I met her. If you hadn't given her the latitude, she'd just have done it without you."

"Yeah," he said. "You're right, I know. But it's not much consolation when a good kid gets killed on my watch."

"She never told you anything about what she was doing?" I asked. "Names, places, times?"

"Nothing," he said. "Just that she was going to Hermosillo to follow up on the guy who got killed in Tucson. Thought there might be some labor angle."

"That's something," I said.

"One day she goes down there," Jameson said. "I don't hear anything for a week. I was worried. That long out of touch, that was extreme, even for her. The next thing I heard was when that Tucson cop called."

"O'Mara," I said.

"Yeah, that was it."

"He called you on his own dime," I said. "It's not TPD's case."

"Doesn't surprise me," Jameson said. "My faith in official channels has never been high, but this really stinks. It's nobody's case."

"You know of anyone she might have confided in? Someone here at SNC or just a friend?"

"I don't think so. She and Jon Cartwright were friends, of course. I think that's why he took the original call for her. But I've been over it with him and everyone else here. They didn't hear from her."

I handed him several business cards. "If you think of someone who might know something useful, please pass these on," I said.

He put one card in his shirt pocket and placed the others on his desk. I stood to leave and thanked him. He rose and shook my hand.

"You know," he said, "the Committee to Protect Journalists called. It's a group that keeps track of attacks on journalists. I couldn't really make it a 'murdered reporter' story for them. I told them that she was working on a story, but I didn't know whether her death was connected to the job. I don't much believe in coincidence, though. Reporter just happens to get raped and murdered when she goes after a story? I don't think so."

"Neither do I," I said.

"I've been doing this for twenty-six years," Jameson said. "I used to think we were being gutsy when we exposed some crooked sewer commissioner or a half-ass movie star screwing a high school cheerleader in the Valley. The courage of the free press. We get full of ourselves sometimes. We forget that there are places where people actually die for this job."

He sat back down, looking even more tired than before. "Good luck," he said. "Let me know if there's anything we can do."

As I made for the door, I looked for the receptionist in the flowery muumuu. I hadn't gotten her name. She was gone, replaced by a gum-chewing girl who kept looking at her watch, or maybe her purple fingernails, as she jotted down messages and fielded phone calls. "Have a nice day," she said, without looking up.

CHAPTER 9

GABRIELA CORONA GAVE ME A HOME ADDRESS FROM SOME KIND OF L.A. big shots directory that listed Robert Lennox. I drove west on Melrose until it ran into Santa Monica Boulevard, then a few more blocks to Lennox's street. If April had been my daughter, I would not be at work now. I would be home, drinking, useless on the job. The rich are different, but it was worth a try.

The house was north of Santa Monica. Lennox's street was modern Beverly Hills, lavish and architecturally schizophrenic. Large but conservative old Federal houses, white with dark green or blue-gray shutters, neighbored new monstrosities of pink stucco with a half-dozen fountains. If the homes had signs in front, one would say GEORGE WASHINGTON SLEPT HERE and the other would say LIVE NUDE GIRLS!

Lennox favored the Federal. On the front step, I found myself standing a bit straighter, wishing I had a hat to hand to the butler.

But, to my surprise, it was Robert Lennox himself who answered the door. He was a tall man, thin and tan, with graying hair in that short, slightly rumpled cut favored by those who passed for old money in Southern California. Lennox was still recognizable from a dusty *Forbes* cover that I found in the library: "Reclusive and resourceful, he quietly expands his global empire," the caption read. I remembered only the headline and picture. The list of his business triumphs was too long to read.

Today, he wore gray slacks and a black wool sweater pulled over a white shirt. His clothes were fresh and his shoes were shined. His hair was combed and his face looked freshly shaved. But like the editor Jameson, his eyes were swollen. His shoulders hunched forward and his head sagged in a way that I couldn't blame on age.

"Mr. Lennox, my name is Brinker. I'm a private investigator from Tucson." I gave him a business card. "I met April shortly before she went to Mexico."

Lennox looked up from the card to me, nodded, and said, "I know your name. April mentioned it to me the last time she called from Tucson. Come in, Mr. Brinker."

He stepped aside as I walked into the entryway. Tucson High could have had a pretty good prom in that hall. A gleaming hardwood floor stretched the length of the house. The ceiling was two stories up, with a crystal chandelier. In the living room, there were no flowers or photographs or signs of any life lived there. One side of the room was an enormous window offering a view of the swimming pool and a large, immaculately kept lawn.

Lennox sat wearily in a dark blue wingback chair. He motioned me to a green sofa. He looked around the room as if he were unfamiliar with it.

"Is this a condolence call?" Lennox asked. "Or are you investigating?"

"Both," I said. "I don't have a client. I'm here on my own behalf. I feel that I let April down because I didn't go with her to Mexico."

"You advised her not to go at all, if I remember correctly," he said.

"Yes."

"Wise counsel, it would seem," he said. "I'm sorry she didn't heed it. Taking advice was never April's strong suit. I begged her not to go down to Mexico. She wouldn't listen. It sounds terrible to say that now, doesn't it? But I think that her willfulness is what people will remember about her."

"Independence," I said. "That's what her editor called it."

"Yes," Lennox said. "She was indeed independent. Now, Mr. Brinker, what do you want from me?"

"I'd like to know anything she told you before she went to Mexico."

"Nothing very useful, I'm afraid. She had a tip to follow, someone to meet, in Hermosillo. She had hoped that you would go with her, but when you declined, she apparently decided to go by herself. Fly down there, she said, but she didn't know when."

"Flying there from Tucson," I said. "That may help. We can get an airline travel record. Did she mention any names or places? Appointments?"

"No," he said. "She knew that the details wouldn't especially interest me. She had just called for the reason she always called. To let me know how she was, and to ask for some money for her travel and other expenses. It was difficult to get advances from that organization she worked for, apparently. I told her that I didn't think she should go there, so I wouldn't underwrite it. But she got the money somehow, or used her credit cards to their limit."

"Mr. Lennox," I said, "April left a message on my machine that said the story had become very important to her. It sounded as though she meant to her, personally. Do you have any idea what she meant?"

He looked out to the great lawn and the pool. "No," he said.

"She didn't say when she planned to come back to the States?"

"No." He turned back to me. "It depended on what she learned in Hermosillo." He stood up and walked to the window, then turned back to me. "A moment ago you said 'we' could find out about April's travel. Who is 'we,' may I ask?"

"I have some friends on a police department," I said, not giving him too much. "They can make requests that don't always work for me."

"And if you find something useful, what then?"

"Then," I said, "I'll follow it up."

"Which would mean," Lennox said, "that you would be going into Mexico and putting yourself in the same sort of danger that April faced. I don't want anyone else to die, Mr. Brinker."

"No disrespect, sir," I said, "but I'll make my own decision and look out for myself."

He straightened from his slump for an instant, startled at the contradiction of his wishes. But he quickly relaxed again and held my eyes as he spoke.

"Point taken," he said. "But you would be wise to consider what I'm telling you. April said she went to investigate a murder, and she was murdered. The nature of the crime leads me to believe that it was committed by a psychopath, not by some conspiracy. But if there is a connection to what she was looking for, why would anyone hesitate to kill you, too?"

"Point taken," I said.

"Why don't you let me use some of the resources available to me?" he said. "I can contact friends in Washington and Sacramento. People with influence on both sides of the border. Perhaps they can move some of the obstinate authorities. Doesn't that make more sense than barging in, making trouble for people who kill?"

"You should do that, for sure," I said. "If you haven't already."

"I have not. I should have. I will now."

"Mr. Lennox," I said, "was an autopsy performed here?"

"No," he said. "That could have been done, obviously, but I decided against it. The Mexican authorities ordered an autopsy. I'm told that it was performed by an excellent physician, even though he's Mexican. He was American-trained, apparently. He reached the obvious conclusion. It seemed worse than pointless to do more. I felt that April had been . . . had been violated enough."

When I did not respond, he said, "You disapprove."

"It's not my place to approve or disapprove," I said. "In a murder case, investigators want all the information they can get. But I can't second-guess you on that."

"You know how this will end," he said. "Some maniac will be caught in the act, or tracked somehow in another crime, and he will confess to harming April. And harming others, too, I wouldn't doubt."

"There have been others," I said. "I need to find out more about those."

I rose and walked toward the door. He followed me. We stood in the high, stark hallway. His voice echoed when he spoke.

"You didn't ask me for money," he said. "Other investigators have come here, you know. They offered to work for me."

"But you didn't hire them."

"No. They're vultures."

"What about me?"

"I don't form hasty opinions, Mr. Brinker," he said. "April liked you. She told me that when she returned from Mexico, she would like to know you better. Did you know that?"

"No, sir. I didn't."

"She was independent in her opinion of men, too, and not altogether fortunate in her choices," Lennox said. "As to you, we shall see."

CHAPTER 10

I DROVE EAST ON SANTA MONICA AND STOPPED AT FATBURGER. THE burgers were pretty good, by fast-food standards, and the name appealed to my sense of political incorrectness. It was early for lunch, so I had my choice of tables. I sat by the window to watch the West Hollywood passing parade. The crowd was young and colorful. They reminded me of April Lennox. I couldn't watch them for long.

I used my cell phone to check for messages at the office in Tucson. The call would not go through. The display panel said REPLACE BATTERY. It had been running down quickly lately. I needed a new one. From the Fatburger window I could see an electronics store about halfway down the block. After lunch, I walked down there and showed a clerk the cell phone.

"Sure," he said. "We've got that one." He scribbled some numbers on an order pad, ripped off the top copy, and started to take it back to the storeroom. A teenager came out of the room just then. My clerk said, "Billy, get me an 8742C, will you? It's on row twelve, in the center, near the top."

Billy gave a little salute and turned around. The clerk said, "Saves me a trip." He wrote up a sales slip and had it totaled when Billy returned with the battery.

Something nagged at me as I left the store. I walked back to Fatburger's parking lot and stood by the rental car, trying to coax the idea from its hiding place. I replayed my conversation with Lennox, my thoughts at lunch, the walk to the electronics store.

It hit me as I drove toward Fairfax for the return trip to the airport. I zipped south to Melrose and back to Southwest News Consortium. Inside, Mama Cass had resumed her post at the desk.

"Hi, again," she said. "Once you've found me, never let me go, right?"

"Darn right," I said. "I didn't get your name before."

"Sandra," she said.

"Were you here, Sandra, taking messages, when April got that call from a woman in Mexico?"

"Oh, no, I would have remembered that," she said. "Ralph and I figured out that Jon Cartwright got that call. He was working at her desk that day."

"You didn't start to write down the message in your book there, then see Jon and ring him?"

"No, no," she said. "Believe me, we've all been over this a thousand times, trying to think of something to help. I never talked to anybody who called from Mexico."

"What about the girl who was here earlier today when you took a break? Could she have taken the call?"

"Hayley? Maybe. She just works part-time. A few hours a week. She's a little spacey, but . . . What day was that, when the call came in?"

We studied her desk calendar and pinpointed the date when the woman called April from Hermosillo. Sandra flipped back through the duplicate pages of her message book.

"There it is," I said. One of the messages said "A.L." on the "for" line. The phone number started 011-52-622, the international long-distance code, the country code for Mexico, and the city code for Hermosillo.

"That's Hayley's writing and her initials at the bottom," Sandra said. "How did you know this would be here?"

"I just saw a guy write an order form that he didn't need, because he spotted someone who could fill it right then. That's what happened here, I'll bet. I think Hayley started to take this message, then spotted Jon Cartwright back at April's desk. So she switched the call to him and probably tossed out the original message slip."

"She might have been nervous because the call came from Mexico. We don't get many from there. She probably wanted to be sure that a reporter got the message. And Jon speaks Spanish. Maybe that was it."

"Sounds likely," I said.

"So, does this help?" Sandra asked.

"This morning, I had zilch," I said. "Now there's a trail to follow."

CHAPTER 11

O'MARA OFFERED TO MAKE THE CALLS, BUT AL SAID, "LET ME DO IT. I can take the heat if somebody upstairs questions why we're calling on a Mexican case." Not many of the brass had stuck their necks out for O'Mara over the years. He nodded his thanks, and looked at Al a little differently after that.

The airline had two daily flights from Tucson to Hermosillo. The first arrived at 11:55 A.M. The returning flight that evening on a tiny commuter plane was fully booked, so April Lennox had asked the airline to reserve a hotel room. The hotel was one of a modern, Mexican-owned chain, located between the airport and downtown. She checked in at 3:42 P.M., according to the computerized front desk records. She made no calls on her room telephone. Nothing indicated where she had dinner. She ate a continental breakfast in the hotel dining room the next morning. At 9:58 A.M., she checked out. She failed to show up at Hermosillo's General Ignacio L. Pesqueira Airport for the morning flight to Tucson and never presented her ticket at another time.

Al looked up from his notes and said, "End of paper trail."

"She must have gone straight from the airport to her meeting with the woman," I said. "Lunch, probably. It was almost four o'clock when she got to the hotel."

"She ate dinner at some nearby restaurant," Al said. "Or maybe she skipped dinner. No restaurant charges on the hotel bill. We'll see about credit card records for the meals."

"Somebody bad picked her up at the hotel the next day," I said. "Unless she took a taxi and it got hijacked."

"We could find out about that," Al said.

"If the hijack was reported," I said.

"Would she be stupid enough to get in a car with somebody she didn't know?" Al said.

"She wasn't stupid at all," I said. "But she was a reporter. The pull of a big story can be irresistible. If she thought she was getting close to something, she might take a chance. Reporters in the Middle East put on blindfolds and ride with strangers to interview terrorists. That *Wall Street Journal* guy in Pakistan was smart and experienced, but he walked into a murder trap."

"Somebody comes up to her at the hotel cab stand and says, 'Oh, *señorita,* I have information on the murder. Come with me, please.' She goes for that?"

"Maybe."

"In over her head," Al said.

"Yes," I said. "I keep thinking of Dolores. What if she had been on this story?"

"Dolores knows the score," Al said. "This April girl, what was her experience down there? A semester abroad in Guadalajara? She probably thinks it's all happy foster families, helping you with your Spanish."

"I have to go to Hermosillo," I said.

Al leaned back in his chair. He kept a baseball on his desk and liked to pick it up, tossing it from hand to hand, when he thought. He'd made a diving catch of that ball when a UCLA batter drove it down the line in right field. The catch ended the inning and saved the game for Arizona. When Al picked himself up, straddling the foul line, he tossed it to the umpire. The ump tossed it back and said, "That's a keeper, son."

Now, rolling the ball in his hands, he said, "We can level with each other, right, *hermano*?"

"Sure," I said.

"I see two possibilities," Al said. "One, this was just what it looks like. A sex crime. The perp sees this pretty American girl and grabs her. If that's it, you have no chance down there. The Mexican police stonewall you, just like cops everywhere do with outsiders. What the hell could you do? Track every known sex offender in Sonora? What if it was this guy's first time? You have nothing to track. Your chance is nil."

"Maybe."

"Not maybe," he said. "For sure. Besides, if it was like that, her death would have no relevant connection to your Juan Doe. Her death would be just ungodly bad luck."

"What's the other possibility?"

"That this is what you think. That whoever clipped our Juan Doe killed her, too. In that case, some serious forces are involved here. They'll have no qualms about killing one more. And the deck is stacked against you down there."

"I may have an ace to pull," I said.

"Oh, brother," Al said. "You mean Hector? You want this that bad?"

"Yes."

Al sighed and said, "Well, *vaya con Dios,* buddy."

CHAPTER 12

Hector Ortiz operated from a restaurant on Avenida Obregón in downtown Nogales, Sonora. It opened when Hector wanted it open. That was usually at night when the tourist trade was too good to ignore, even for a guy whose principal occupation was sating the borderland appetite for drugs.

Two couples stood outside as I approached. One of the men was wiggling the door and peering inside. He wore a shiny red shirt patterned with yellow hula girls in short grass skirts.

"Smells great in there," he said. He spoke with that almost southern twang that you sometimes hear in Kansas. "But they're not open yet."

"It's lunchtime," one of the women said. "They must be opening soon."

I stood by the glass panel in the door's center. One of Hector's men saw me and opened up.

"Ah!" said the tourist. "Perfect timing. We're in luck."

I stepped inside and Hector's guy put his bulk in the doorway, blocking the tourists. He was about six-foot-three and had rippling muscular arms with the girth of pythons.

"Abrimos a las seis," he said, giving them an obsequious smile. He held up six fingers, then tapped the face of his watch. *"A las seis. Muchas gracias.* Plis to be combing bock. *Muchas gracias."*

The tourists moved away. The other woman said, "My goodness, they must cook all day for dinner."

Hector's guy locked the door behind us and said, "Dumb shits. You see that shirt? Wear that in Hawaii, Five-0 would bust him on a felony."

"Jack Lord's dead," I said.

"That shirt would bring him out of his grave, man. The boss is in the dining room. My name is Vicente and I'll be your frisker today. Put out your arms, Brinker."

He patted me down, although we both knew that I would not carry a weapon in here. With Mexico's strict, hypocritical gun laws, only a fool would bring one into the country. Only a suicidal fool would carry one into this building.

Hector sat at his usual table in the empty dining room. He had the bench seat with his back to the wall with the big, colorful *serape* on it. One of his men stood by the rear door. Another leaned against the kitchen entrance.

"You're just in time for lunch," Hector said. He held up a tequila bottle. "I figure you'll skip the *menudo,* so we'll get right to the main course."

"Tripe has never been my favorite," I said.

"*Gringo* sensibilities," he said. "You don't know what you're missing."

I last saw him more than a year ago. He still hadn't aged much from the teenage shortstop I watched play in Tucson high school games. The black hair stayed abundant and dark. His moustache had been trimmed a bit since its Pancho Villa days. In his business, practitioners killed each other every week, but he looked relaxed and untroubled.

He poured a glass of burnt golden tequila and pushed it across the table to me.

"How's business?" I said.

"Can't keep up with demand," he said. "How's your friend Avila?"

"Good," I said.

"Still got the arm?"

"Not bad. These days, I don't know if he could throw a really fast guy out at the plate."

Hector laughed. "Good cutoff man like me at shortstop, we could get it done."

I drank the shot of tequila and put down the glass. I said, "I need your help, Hector. I don't like to ask, but I need it."

"You don't like to ask," he said.

"I'm probably breaking some law just talking to you," I said.

"I am what I am," he said. "But we took turns keeping each other alive, *amigo*. I don't think that was against the law, either time."

"A guy got killed at Lovers Crossing," I said.

"Didn't count," Hector said. "He was an asshole."

He poured us each another glass of tequila and said, "So, what do you need?"

"An American woman, a reporter named April Lennox, was murdered down here," I said.

"I heard," he said.

"I want to know what happened. And I want to know who did it."

Hector thought about that, took a sip of tequila, and said, "Then what?"

"Then," I said, "I'll figure out what to do."

"Justice," he said.

"Yes," I said.

He put down his glass and laughed softly. "You guys are too much," he said. "You sit up there in the land of the free and the home of the brave, all smug, talking about rights and democracy and shit. You figure we're just a bunch of Mexican crooks and peons. But you want somebody aced, you don't mind coming down here to get it done."

"I didn't say anything about killing," I said.

Hector smiled and said, "Right." He poured another drink into the shot glass. He put it on the table and tapped his fingers beside it. I could hear the overhead fans whirring, and pots clanking in the kitchen, somebody laughing out on the street.

"I heard about that girl," Hector said. "I made some calls. An American gets killed down here and what do people think? That it had something to do with my business. So I like to keep informed. I called the guys who usually have news for me on, uh, law enforcement issues. They're reliable because I make it worth their while. And they said, don't worry about it. Nobody suspects my associates were involved. But that's all they would say. There's a pretty heavy lid on information about this."

"Even you can't learn anything more?" I asked.

"Well," he said, "when I heard that I'm getting no heat, I forgot about it. Now you come down here asking questions and I'm wondering if I don't know something I should."

Hector nodded to the guard by the kitchen. The guard opened the door and spoke to someone inside. A moment later, a cook emerged with two plates. He brought them to the table. It was steak *a la Tampiqueña,* a thin slice of grilled beef surrounded by onions, guacamole, a cheese enchilada, and refried beans. It was probably a week's worth of nutrition for some people living in the *colonias,* barely a mile from here.

"So what should I know?" Hector said.

I ate a piece of steak. It wasn't as good as La Fuente's in Tucson, but I decided not to tell Hector.

"A guy got murdered at the basketball riot," I said. "April Lennox thought he had come to Tucson to give her a story. She arranged to meet a relative of the victim in Hermosillo. That's where we lost her trail. There's nothing from the time she checked out of the hotel in Hermosillo until her body was found here."

Hector took a very small sip of tequila.

"Who moves a body two hundred and sixty kilometers?" he said.

"Two possibilities," I said. "One, she wasn't dead. She had to be brought to Nogales for some reason. Questioning, maybe. I don't even want to think about that. Two, they killed her in Hermosillo. Whoever did it tried to put some distance between himself and the murder. Or throw suspicion onto someone in Nogales."

"That's the part that bothers me," Hector said.

"But you know that the cops don't suspect you."

"Not yet, they don't. If this starts getting attention and they need a patsy, I might be their choice. I buy insurance policies, but you never know when a higher bidder comes along."

"Can you find out about the autopsy? Everyone in the States gets told it was a sex crime."

"We been having those," Hector said. "More than you've heard about. Some pretty ugly shit. Maybe that's what happened."

"Sure," I said.

"Okay, maybe not," he said. "Let me see what I can find out. Like I told you, though, information's not exactly gushing."

"The other thing I want to know is what happened at the hotel in Hermosillo. If I go down there and start questioning bellhops and doormen, I'll be way too obvious. You got anybody who could ask some discreet questions?"

"Maybe," he said. "What hotel?"

I told him and he nodded.

"Can you trace a Mexican phone number?" I said.

"It'll take two or three minutes of hard work," he said.

I gave him the number that April Lennox had called. He wrote it down on the paper place mat.

"Thanks for lunch, Hector," I said.

"Got flan for dessert," he said.

I shook my head and made for the door.

CHAPTER 13

Jon Cartwright called from Colorado. He said he had a two-hour layover in Phoenix on his way home to L.A. He offered to meet me at the coffee shop outside security in the America West terminal. I headed up I-10, doing eighty in the slow lane. I rolled into Sky Harbor twenty minutes early.

I spotted him as he came out of the concourse. He had told me to watch for jeans, a faded plaid shirt, and brown hair pulled back in a short ponytail. The hair looked a little gray to me, but maybe he didn't see it.

"Mr. Cartwright?" I said.

"Brinker," he said, putting out his hand. "I'm trying to remember the last time somebody called me Mister. Make it Jon."

I bought the coffees and we sat by a window overlooking the terminal entrance road. We seemed to be the only two people not talking on cell phones.

"I don't know what I can tell you," he said. "You got the number of the woman in Hermosillo, right?"

"Yes," I said. "We haven't traced it yet, but that's a place to start."

"So," he said.

"So, I was hoping you could tell me something about April. We've assumed that she was killed because of the story."

"The murdered guy in Tucson?"

"Yes," I said. "But maybe not. Was anybody mad at her? Was she afraid of something?"

He smiled. "April wasn't afraid of much."

"I figured," I said. "Your editor told me that she was following up on the murder in Tucson, and there might be a labor angle."

"She never told me," he said. "That sounds like her, though. If she could tie some third world guy's murder to a corrupt boss, she'd love that. Honest laborer exploited by vicious capitalist. Yeah, she'd want that story."

"Well, that's just a guess. We know there's a run of sex crimes in Nogales. She might have been caught up in that."

"I hate to think about that," he said.

"She left a message on my answering machine," I said. "She claimed the story had turned personal for her. She seemed to emphasize that. 'Important to me,' she said. You have any idea what that was about?"

"No," Cartwright said. "But lots of stories were personal to her. One hungry kid, one screwed-over worker someplace. It's like I say. She had the passion for that stuff."

"Maybe so," I said.

"She had passion to spare," he said, smiling. "How long did you know her?"

"Three or four days," I said.

Cartwright nodded. "Then you slept with her."

He caught my surprise and laughed.

"Not all that startling a conclusion," he said. "She'd have liked you. You're kind of clean-cut, and strong-looking. And you're, uh, a little older than she was."

"I didn't sleep with her," I said. "Not how you're thinking."

"Have it your way," he said.

"And how did you come by this insight about her?" I said.

He shrugged and smiled.

"She couldn't resist you, huh?" I said.

"I'm not bragging," he said. "Especially now, after what happened to her. She was April, Brinker. That's just a fact."

"Okay," I said.

"I don't care if you believe me or not," he said. He leaned in close. "But let me ask you this. Did she cry in the night? Did she grab on to your pillow in the morning like she was afraid you'd leave her there?"

I thought about putting a right hook into his nose, but two Phoenix cops sat down at a table only ten feet away.

"You got time for a beer?" I said.

WE WENT TO THE BAR ON THE NORTH SIDE OF THE TERMINAL. IT WAS pretty early for drinking, so we had a quiet corner to ourselves. The waitress brought us two bottles of Dos Equis.

"If beer were the biggest factor in quality of life," Cartwright said, "I'd move to Mexico."

"Why would you tell me this stuff about April?" I said.

"You asked me," he said. "You want to know if something about her got her killed. I'm just telling you this. That girl wanted to be close to a man. No, not wanted. Needed. And she looked so good, she never had any trouble finding one."

"You think somebody she hooked up with killed her?"

"I have no clue," he said. "It's not like she'd go find a biker bar or a crack house just to get a guy."

"She was selective," I said, probably sounding hopeful.

Cartwright picked up on it and laughed. "She lived in L.A., man," he said. "There are plenty of guys to be selective with."

"Anybody in particular?" I said.

He sat back and took a drink of beer and looked around the room. I see this often when people talk to a detective. They're thinking, How much can I tell him? Can I get hurt by opening up to this guy?

"There was one," he said. He leaned forward and spoke very softly. "When April and I were together, she told me that she wanted to stay clear of her last boyfriend. When she broke it off with him, he made threats."

"Serious threats?"

"April didn't know. But she just didn't want to deal with him."

"What did he say?"

"Like, 'Nobody dumps me, you bitch.' He said he'd make her pay."

"Just tough-guy talk?" I said. "Face-saving when she left him?"

"More than that," Cartwright said. "She told me that he'd been rough with her before."

"How rough?" I asked.

"Rough enough that she didn't come to work for a week. And

she was skittish about men for a while after that. I know, because I was next."

A middle-aged couple walked in, looked around the bar, and walked out.

"Who's the guy?" I said.

"His name was Dickie Ungerlieder," he said.

"No wonder he was violent," I said.

"It's not the name. It's the money," he said. "Dickie was born with a pile of it. He thinks it gives him the right to treat people however he wants. The queen of England could walk in, and Dickie would make her feel inferior."

"You ever see him get physical with anyone?"

"Nah. I only met him once. He's a private kind of bully, you know? April said he realizes that he's being an asshole, so he doesn't let anybody see. In public, he's not violent. Just obnoxious."

"When did you meet him?"

"Before April and I got together. Her father's company had a big party at the Beverly Hills Hotel. She got invites for a few of us at SNC. Dickie was her date. Later she told me that she brought him just to freak out her father. And she wanted to see if Dickie could hold his own in that classy crowd. But he did okay. Mingled with the swells. Didn't use the wrong fork or praise a Democrat or anything. April said he even schmoozed some potential investors for one of his cockamamie investment deals."

"Where do I find this sweetheart?" I asked.

"Malibu," Cartwright said. "He has a couple of other homes, I think. But he spends most of his time there. Got the beach and the L.A. scene and plenty of coke. Everything a rich jerk needs."

He took a pencil from his shirt pocket and wrote something on a cocktail napkin. He pushed it across to me. It was an address on Pacific Coast Highway.

"I took April out there to get some of her stuff," he said. "I don't go to houses on the ocean side of PCH often, so I remember the address."

We sat for a few minutes, drinking our beers, until Cartwright looked at his watch. "I better get back," he said. "Don't want to miss the flight."

"She had so much going for her," I said. "You wonder how she could get messed up with guys like that."

"You met the old man?" he said. I wanted to ask him what he meant, but he was up and trotting toward the gates.

CHAPTER 14

I PLUNGED TWO DOS EQUIS BOTTLES INTO A BUCKET OF ICE AND carried it to the back patio. It was a perfect Arizona springtime night. The air still held its warmth from the afternoon sun, a sign of summer's approach. A breeze moved the palo verde branches. The tops of cedars swayed.

The phone rang. When I answered, Gabriela Corona said, "No time for music trivia tonight, babe. Got information for you. Not much, though."

"Let's hear it," I said. "You never know what helps."

"I pulled up summaries of fifty stories by April Lennox. It looks like she started at SNC about three years ago. She wrote every three weeks or so, give or take. The various alt-weeklies could run the stories or not. Most of them took everything."

"Papers in Arizona and California?" I asked.

"Mainly those," Gabi said. "Her stories tended to be in California, so that's a logical fit."

"Okay," I said.

"I didn't see anything about Mexico in the summaries. Some stories you could call Hispanic-related, I suppose. Farm labor exploitation in the Imperial Valley and up north of Fresno. She did one about Latino U.S. citizens being hassled over their voting rights in Orange County. But she never filed from Mexico, or did a story about Mexico, as far as I can tell."

"Oppression and murder, she said to me once," I said. "The guy meeting her wanted to talk about oppression and murder. He had read her some of her stories and chose her because of that."

"Well, the labor stories would qualify, I suppose," she said. "They had the usual SNC, alt-weekly slant. Greedy conglomerate farm executives, noble toilers in the fields, viva César Chávez stuff. She did some decent reporting, actually. But I guess a worker who felt oppressed would like them."

"Thanks, Gabi."

"*De nada,* buddy. One more thing. She had nothing on record with LAPD or county sheriffs. And she never filed a complaint or requested a court order, like to deal with a stalker."

"I didn't think of that," I said.

"That's because you're not an astonishingly beautiful yet vulnerable woman. We worry about that stuff all the time." Gabi could say something like that because, mistakenly, she never thought of herself as attractive.

"Anyway," she said, "it was worth a check. But you and I know this wasn't a nut job. Somebody wanted to shut her up before she got a story out."

"So I have to find an undiscovered story," I said.

Gabi laughed. "Join the club," she said. "And don't forget, I have dibs when you come up with any actual facts."

"Might be a while," I said.

"I can wait," she said. "It's what I do best."

AT TEN-THIRTY, THE DOORBELL RANG. I HAD A PEEPHOLE CAMERA IN the front door connected to a monitor in the coat closet. Paranoia runs deep, and I had installed new security after a bad former colleague on the Border Patrol decided that I was expendable. Now Hector's man, the guy with the big muscles and a distaste for loud Hawaiian shirts, smiled into the camera. I opened the door.

"From the boss," he said. He handed me a letter-sized manila envelope. "He thinks his cell phones are a little risky these days."

"How did you get across the border?" I asked.

"I'm a natural-born U.S. citizen, Brinker," he said. "No police agency anywhere wants me for anything. I come and go like a tourist."

"Want a drink?"

"Thanks. Rain check. Got a Tucson *señorita* I like to visit when I'm up here. Don't want to keep her waiting."

"Tell Hector I appreciate this."

"He knows," the man said. He turned and walked back to a Chevy Suburban with Arizona plates and a highly polished black finish that gleamed in the starlight.

I grabbed a third beer from the fridge and returned to the patio. The manila envelope was filled with pages from a lined legal tablet. On the first page, Hector wrote in a large hand that used two lines:

Looks like your girl was set up. She checked out of the hotel, like you told me, and got a cab at the front door. There were three doormen and bellhops on duty that morning. They remembered her because they don't see many pretty blond gringas *there by themselves. It's usually couples or tourist girls in flocks. The guys all kidded the doorman who pushed them out of the way to help her, even though she had just a little carry bag. The doorman's name was Pablo Carillo. My guys got this from both the other doormen. They say it's good information.*

My heart was pounding. A guy falling over everyone to help April Lennox didn't seem strange. Plenty of guys would. But Hector was leading up to something. I took a drink of beer and turned the page.

Carillo had worked there for a year or so. He was just a regular guy, everybody said. He was always borrowing money until the next payday, though. So maybe a little extra money would lead him to break the rules.

From the start, Hector's handwriting was hard to read. At this point, he seemed to be writing faster.

*When he took her bag, he called up a cab that was waiting on the left side of the entrance road, instead of the right side, where all the other cabs were. He put her in that one and said, '*Aeropuerto.*' The other* *cabbies gave him grief about it, but he laughed it off. He said she was so beautiful that he got confused. He said he'd buy them all a beer later. Nobody got the cab number. It was probably phony anyway. There is no cab dispatch record or videotaped security camera at the hotel entrance.*

I drank more of my beer and went to the next page.

We know that April never made the airport. The next morning, Carillo did not show up for work. There is no phone where he lives, so the manager went to his apartment building and asked around. Carillo lived by himself. He had not said anything about leaving or quitting his job. The manager figured he was hung over or maybe overslept at some puta *place. It happens. But it has been almost three weeks now. Carillo never came back.*

On the last page, Hector wrote:

The phone number you gave me comes back to Jorge Esposito, 82 *Calle de la República, Hermosillo.* Buena suerte, amigo.

Down near the bottom, like an afterthought, he had scribbled:

No sex crime or random carjack. Your girl was taken out on purpose by professionals.

CHAPTER 15

ALEJANDRO AND KATZ LEASED ACCESS TO AN ONLINE NEWS SERVICE at the law office. I logged on and searched for recent murders in Mexico. The wires, newspapers, and magazines had covered multiple homicides in Ciudad Juárez, across the Rio Grande from El Paso, and in Nogales.

In Juárez, as many as thirty young women had been murdered by an apparent serial killer. The police made arrests and claimed to have confessions, but evidence was weak. Victims' families suspected political motivation in the investigations.

Nogales was different. Officials connected a couple of the ten killings there, but treated most as isolated crimes. Without the serial angle, the newspapers did nothing to play up the stories. But as O'Mara thought, the victims did have much in common: all young women, some of them workers at the *maquiladoras,* the foreign-owned assembly plants, in and around Nogales. A couple were prostitutes, at least according to the police statements. All had been sexually attacked. Most, unlike April Lennox, were killed with knives.

I called Miguel Calderón, the U.S. Consulate officer in Nogales who had spoken to Tommy O'Mara. He remembered my name from the business card in April's pocket. He said that he would be available for a half hour at three o'clock.

For the second time in two days, I headed down I-19 to Nogales. The parking lot attendant remembered me. I paid the fee and tipped him to keep an eye on the car, then hiked a couple of blocks to the pedestrian border crossing.

We called the checkpoint a choke point. All the traffic between the U.S. and Mexico was squeezed into a few heavily guarded crossings. The government claimed that its policy allowed greater control of immigration, but it also forced many illegal crossers out to the brutal desert, where they fell to bandits and rattlesnakes and killer summer sun.

Auto traffic was backed up beyond the Pemex gas station, probably to the railroad tracks a mile away. Commercial truckers at the other crossing were squeezed even worse. The delays had doubled since the 9/11 terrorist attacks.

I walked down the narrow passage by the Customs building and pushed through the turnstile. The shiver kicked in, the one that always hits me when I step across that line. I took a breath and started toward Avenida Obregón, the main drag.

Hector's man was browsing at the bookstore and newsstand near the border crossing. I had not been there in years, but I remembered that the store specialized in paperback romances. It was frequented by teenagers and young women. Hector's man seemed out of place there. It was a good watcher's spot, though. It sat on a corner, with doors on rollers that pushed open to give browsers a full view of both streets. Hector's man gave no sign of noticing me. He was still there, thumbing through the bodice rippers, when I turned the corner.

It had to be coincidence. Hector wasn't having me watched. He had no reason even to know that I was coming back today. Coincidence, for sure.

The consulate was strategically positioned between Avenida Obregón and Boulevard Luis Donaldo Colosio, the main roads to the border crossings. It was near several small industrial parks, the bus station, and a Burger King. It's a small world after all.

Calderón met me in the lobby. He was young and buttoned down in a blue broadcloth shirt, conservative striped tie, dressy khakis, and cordovan penny loafers. I made him for an MBA with international trading concentration, looking for a ride out of Nogales to Foggy Bottom.

"Not much I can tell you," he said when we sat in his small office, "but I do have one thing that you'll probably want to see." He passed me a file folder that said LENNOX, APRIL on the tab. I opened it and saw that it was an autopsy report.

"No pictures," Calderón said. "I thought I'd spare you that. I'm told that she was a friend."

"This is in English," I said.

"The medical examiner wrote it in both languages," he said. "He's a Sonora native and a graduate of UCLA Medical School. I did look over both versions. The translation is precise. It's what you already know, Mr. Brinker."

"Cause of death, manual strangulation? Sexual assault?"

"Yes," he said. "The assault was antemortem, incidentally. They don't know how long, but they think it was well before the infliction of the fatal injuries. You'll find that the autopsy was conducted very thoroughly and professionally. Dr. Macias is a very fine man."

"How about the crime scene investigation?" I said.

"Ah," Calderón said. "That's something else."

"How so?"

"For one thing," he said, "no one seems to know how long Ms. Lennox's body was at the location where it was found. The autopsy places time of death at two days previous. Therefore, no one knows if or how much the crime scene was disturbed between the time the body was placed there and the time it was found. So even a first-class investigation by U.S. standards would be handicapped by the circumstances."

"And this wasn't a first-class investigation," I said.

"I'm not a law enforcement man, Mr. Brinker," he said. "This consulate is largely a business facilitation office, and we handle visas, of course. So I am no expert on crime investigations."

"But?"

"But, just between you and me, they do things differently here. Local police handled the initial matters. State Judicial Police took over because of the seriousness of the crime and the need for coordinated investigation. When it became clear, largely from your information, that Ms. Lennox was a United States citizen, Mexico City apparently got involved."

"Apparently?"

"I say that because it's not entirely clear. You want to waste a month, go from agency to agency in the Mexican bureaucracy, trying to get information. Believe me, it makes Washington look like a model of efficiency."

A photograph on his desk showed him, a pretty young Hispanic woman with short dark hair and a warm smile, and a boy and girl who looked like little copies of Mom and Dad. The family was standing at the entrance to the Heard Museum in Phoenix.

"Where are you from?" I said.

"Peoria," he said. "Arizona, not Illinois. I joined the State Department to see the world. Here I am, in a distant, exotic land."

"Probably hoping for the Paris Embassy," I said.

"I'd settle for Latvia," he said. "Beats farm labor, though. My family's occupational background. When my father was forty, he could barely stand up. He'd have my mother rub his back and he'd say to me, 'You're an American. Go to college.'"

"That reminds me of something," I said. "April Lennox did stories on labor conflicts with Mexican angles. Anything strange going on with the *maquiladoras* here? Or maybe mining or some other industry?"

"Strange?"

"April said the man who called her talked about a story of oppression and murder. I'm wondering if there's bad labor trouble that somebody wanted to keep a lid on."

"Well," Calderón said, "I don't know much about mines, but I can tell you all about *maquiladoras*. And I can refer you to someone who knows even more."

He opened the top drawer of his desk and produced a business card. "Carl Brooks," he said. "Carl is the manager for several U.S.-owned businesses down here. You should talk to him."

"Thanks," I said.

"Sure," he said. "The *maquiladoras* are a big part of my job. Look out here."

He rose and walked to the one window in his office. He opened the louvered blinds to allow a view outside.

"We have about a hundred of them here in Nogales. They employ thirty-two thousand people, give or take. That's a pretty big deal in a city of two hundred thousand people."

He pointed to a sprawling sheet metal building a few hundred yards down the road.

"That one there makes plastic knobs and handles for cars. They supply several of the major automakers. Five hundred people work in there."

"Five hundred people making little knobs and handles?" I said.

"Yep. The world's automobile industry needs a lot of them. And here's why they come to Nogales. If those five hundred people are doing that work in Detroit or Van Nuys or wherever, they earn forty, fifty thousand a year. Maybe more, with union benefits and all. You know what they make here?"

"Let me guess," I said. "Less."

"A lot less," Calderón said. "Most of them get sixty to a hundred dollars a week. That's maybe three thousand to five thousand dollars a year. And you don't have a lot of labor disputes. That's a good wage down here. And no environmental hassles. Mexico is a very employer-friendly country."

"So a U.S. company saves ninety percent on labor."

"Right. There are some unique expenses involved in setting up a factory here. Moving equipment or buying it new. Transporting goods to be assembled. Arranging leases here, when perhaps the company owned property in the States. Buyout expenses for the existing U.S. labor force, maybe, if they're unionized. But basically, it's a bonanza."

"So," I said, "if people were trying to upset this nice little setup, they might provoke a reaction?"

He laughed. "What, some corporate assassin would shoot them from the grassy knoll? Sounds a little conspiratorial to me. Mr. Brinker, nobody wants to upset this setup except the AFL-CIO. NAFTA is the law. Free trade is the reality, and there's no going back to protectionism, at least not in North America. The companies love it. And the workers know they're in competition with, say, China and India. We're already losing jobs to them. People there will work for even less."

"How many of the ten women killed down here worked at the *maquiladoras*?" I said.

Calderón pursed his lips and stared out the window. He turned and looked for a moment at the picture of his wife and children. He drew a deep breath before facing me.

"Just between you and me?" he said.

"Okay."

"Seven," he said. "And the others had connections. But that's all you get on that one, *señor.* I'm late for my three-thirty."

CHAPTER 16

I LEFT THE CONSULATE, BYPASSED BURGER KING, AND WALKED NORTH on Avenida Obregón toward the border. Two blocks from the consulate, the sidewalk zigged around a Pemex gas station, cutting off my view of the street. Hector's man stepped out and said, "*Buenas tardes*, Brinker."

"Me and my shadow," I said. This time it was no coincidence. "Vicente, was it?"

"Yeah, that'll do. Sounds presidential." He spoke softly in a mellow bass voice that reminded me of many American Indians I know. The muscles in his arms and chest stretched his golf shirt.

"You tailing me for some reason, Vicente?"

He nodded in the direction of the border. "I'm not tailing you," he said. "I'm tailing someone else."

"And who would that be?"

"The tourist with the discount Hawaiian shirt and his buddy. Remember them?"

"From the other day at Hector's?"

"While you were talking with the boss, I was out in the waiting area out front. When I closed the doors, those guys and the women wandered off. But they kept coming back, up and down the street. Real tourists maybe go up the street on one side, come back on the other. But nobody does it for an hour, back and forth, you know? So we decided to keep an eye on them."

"And?"

"Turns out," Vicente said, "they're tailing you."

"How do you know?" I said.

"They followed you home yesterday," he said. "One of my guys followed them. They left when you got to your house and looked like you're in for the night."

"So you had no problem coming up last night with Hector's message."

"Right. But they were back on you when you left this afternoon. You might want to keep a little sharper eye out. One of the women tailed you to Green Valley, according to my guy who tailed her."

"A regular convoy," I said.

"We figure she called somebody here. Told them you were headed for the border. That's how the tourists were in place when you walked across. I was watching them when you spotted me at the bookstore."

Pretty good, I thought.

"You need to get moving," Vicente said. "When they saw you

leave the consulate, they split. Probably figured you'd be headed up to the Port of Entry to go home."

"I am."

"So they're a step ahead of you. Remember that. They'll be expecting you to cross pretty soon. If they plan to stick with you tonight, they'll have somebody pick you up on the other side."

"Where do you think they came from?" I said.

"Beats me," he said. "But it's got to be about the dead girl. You got no other reason to be here. I don't think they're tagging along to help you."

I WATCHED FOR TAILS AS I SPED UP THE INTERSTATE FROM NOGALES to Tucson. One vehicle seemed to play tag with me, pulling ahead, slowing down, easing ahead again. It was hard to feel suspicious about a van full of seniors from Two Nations Travel, though. They took the exit at Tubac.

At the Border Patrol's I-19 checkpoint, I got the Anglo driver's usual wave-through. Even before I reached him, the young agent was looking beyond me to the next car. It appeared to be carrying a Hispanic family. They were ordered to pull over for closer inspection. There was no vehicle behind that one.

Baggins on Oracle was still open, so I bought a turkey sandwich and took it home. I grabbed a beer from the refrigerator and carried my dinner out to the back patio. The day's warmth had eased to that magical Arizona point that feels like no temperature at all. The neighborhood was silent except for the cooing of doves and the occasional distant bark of a family dog.

I closed my eyes and imagined a living April Lennox going

about her work, embracing life and kicking crass capitalist butt, smiling at me and saying, "Your loss." I wondered what made her cry in the night as she clutched at a piece of worn leather on an ancient sofa.

April's image disappeared when the phone rang.

"Guess what?" Vicente said. "Up your street, west, a white Camry. One male inside. Looks like one of our tourists from yesterday. He's been there about a half hour. He's got a good view of your driveway. You want me to have a talk with him?"

"I'll do it," I said.

"Your call," he said. "But sooner or later, my boss wants to know what's going on here."

"Okay," I said.

I grabbed my pistol and put on a shoulder holster and a jacket to cover it. I walked through the side fence and across my neighbor's yard. He and his family were visiting relatives in San Diego. The back of his property opened to a street that circled around to the neighborhood's main road. I walked along that one until I came to my own street.

From the corner, I could see the rear end of the white Camry. It was parked about halfway to my driveway on the undeveloped side of the road. I calculated that I could get to the car without being seen. The ground on that side was brushy, with a few palo verdes and even two fat saguaro cacti. The sun was down now, and the moon was still low in the sky and faint.

I stepped off the road onto the rough ground. It was dry and rocky, but I walked lightly and made almost no sound. I heard a hiss from somewhere up the hill and froze. There had to be rattlesnakes out here. But it kept hissing rhythmically, and I realized that a lawn sprinkler had just come on at a house behind me. As I approached the car, I could see the man sitting low, staring toward my driveway. The engine was not running, which meant no air conditioner. Which meant the windows, at least the driver's window, could be down. I angled a little deeper into the brush to have a better look at the sides of the car. Both front windows were down.

If the doors were locked, I could open one with the interior handle. Toyota. Anna drove one. I tried to remember how the door handles worked. Fairly high on the front of the interior door panel. Logic dictated pulling back on the handle to release the lock and open the door. I could not take a chance on the outside door handle. That might give the driver just enough time to get the drop on me.

I squatted down and duck-walked parallel to the car for the last twenty feet. That gave me a nice cover of brush to approach the right front door. I rose a few inches and peeked long enough to see the driver, still sitting low behind the wheel, and looking a little sleepy. I drew my pistol and crept up to the door. I knelt at the midpoint of the door. This wouldn't work, I realized, with the gun in my right hand. I needed that hand to open the door. I switched the gun, stood quickly, reached in and grabbed the door handle, pulled it, stepped behind the opening door, and slid into the passenger seat. The guy looked at me and the pistol pointed at his head.

"Easy, pal," he said.

"It sure was," I said. "Hands on the top of the wheel, *pal.*"

His hands shook as he put them there. Little spots of perspiration appeared on his forehead. He looked way too young for this, and plenty scared. He wore a T-shirt with a picture of Meat Loaf and a fiery logo that said BAT OUT OF HELL 25th ANNIVERSARY TOUR. The kid could not have been born when that album came out. There was no gun in sight.

"I want to know why you're following me and who put you up to it," I said.

"Might be worse if I tell you than if I don't," he said.

"Might not," I said.

"Oh, fuck this," he said. "You're gonna shoot me on your own street with your own gun? Like, we're sitting together in a car and I'm a menace to society or something? Jesus, Brinker, you might just as well drive straight downtown and surrender your license." A little break in his voice betrayed the bravado.

"Start the engine and put up the windows," I said. I pulled up the emergency brake handle.

"What?" he said.

"Do it," I said. "Move the right hand very slowly toward the keys. When it starts, put your hand back up on the wheel."

He did it.

"Now," I said, "the left hand, very slowly to the window switches. When the windows are up, put the left back up on the wheel."

He did it. He was sweating a little more now.

I moved the gun around in front of his face.

"It's a small gun," I said. I moved the barrel close to his right hand and pressed it against the little finger. "Probably wouldn't stop an angry linebacker. But inside a closed car, with the motor running, well, you know what they say. If a gun goes off and nobody hears it, did it make a sound?"

"Jesus, Brinker," he said. "You're crazy."

"Course, we'll hear it," I said.

"This is nuts, man," he said. "I'm just hired help."

"Probably don't even have workers' comp," I said. I wiggled the barrel just a bit on his finger.

"C'mon, Brinker." He was shaking now, and there was a sour smell in the front seat. "What do you want from me?"

"Here's the deal," I said. "You're such an amateur, I believe you are low on the food chain. So if you want to drive away from here with a full hand of fingers, point me up. Tell me who's your boss and how I find him."

"Sam Doyle," he said. "Security office on East Twelfth Street, near Park. Okay?"

I pushed the pistol a little harder against his hand. "What does he say the job's about?"

"He didn't say. I don't ask. We just chase you down to Mexico and back. We see who you talk to. I tell Sam. That's it. Nobody's looking to hurt you, man."

I hit the button to lower my window. I opened the door and eased out of the car, keeping the gun trained on him. I closed the door and leaned through the open window.

"Anybody sneaking around after me, I figure that he is looking to hurt me. You're off the job, *pal.* Spread the word. Next time I catch one of you clowns, it won't be a game. Get off my street."

I didn't have to tell him twice. He put the car in gear and sped into the gathering gloom. I memorized the license plate number.

CHAPTER 17

ARIZONA'S DEPARTMENT OF PUBLIC SAFETY LICENSES PRIVATE investigators. Its Web site had no listing for Sam Doyle in Tucson or anywhere else in the state. The next morning, I called Phoenix and got a reasonably live person at DPS to check. No Doyle.

The Tucson phone book had no listing in the residential or business white pages for Sam Doyle. There was one S. Doyle, but I recognized the address from a past missing persons case. It was a retirement community on the east side. I found no Doyle in the yellow pages under private investigators or security.

I checked the Pima County Assessor Web site. No Sam, Samuel, or S. Doyle was on the property tax rolls. I Googled the name and came up with a cattle rancher in Texas, a Pontiac dealer in Michigan, and a candidate for provincial parliament in Ontario, Canada.

O'Mara ran the Camry's license plate. It came back to a box number at an East Broadway Boulevard address.

"It's a print shop and mailbox service," he said. "You could stake it out, I suppose."

"The guy might only come in once a month," I said.

"Well, here's the good news. Broadway is only a block away from East Twelfth Street. And that block is just east of Park. So maybe that kid told you the truth about Doyle having an office there."

"I'll check it," I said. "I have another possibility, too. Somebody I helped once."

Sharon Kruke was a single mother whose teenage daughter Joanne ran off to Los Angeles three years ago. It had taken me about an hour to track down the girl. I had driven over there, picked her up, and brought her home.

Home wasn't much. Mother and daughter lived in a tiny apartment near 22nd Street and Kino Parkway. Sharon drove a ten-year-old Ford that looked ready for the wrecker. I said that she didn't have to pay me. "Yes, I do," she said in a proud voice that brooked no disagreement. She sent me a few dollars every week for two years.

Now I called her office at Tucson City Hall.

"Name it," she said, when I told her that I could use a favor.

I gave her Sam Doyle's name and asked her to check for any business with the city.

"Our databases aren't very well coordinated," she said. "I'll have to run several checks. But I could get you city tax information, permits applied for and issued, building code violations, if he has any."

"That would be perfect, Sharon," I said.

"You know what? Joanne graduated from high school in May. She got a job at the Recorder's Office. I can have her check voter registration, too."

"How's she doing?"

"Terrific. You wouldn't believe it, Mr. Brinker. I think she saw that the bright lights aren't all that bright when you have no money. When your so-called friends just want to, y'know, use you. She really turned it around."

Runaway stories didn't always end that well.

"I'm glad, Sharon," I said. "Give her my best. I don't think she liked me the day I brought her back, but maybe she changed her mind."

"She did. I guarantee it. I'll call you as soon we check the databases."

I made a small pot of coffee, scrambled two eggs, and had my breakfast while I read the morning newspaper. Sharon called before I had finished the sports section.

"Nothing," she said. "Mr. Doyle is not running a business or paying sales taxes or applying for permits in the city of Tucson. I'm sorry, Mr. Brinker. I wish I could give you more help."

"You have helped," I said. "I have a little better idea what I'm dealing with."

"Well, good. Call me anytime you need something. And Joanne says hello. I was right. She does like you."

SO MUCH FOR HIGH-TECH AND PERSONAL CONNECTIONS. AS DOLORES says, sometimes you just have to get off your butt and go knock on doors.

I drove south, past the university and Tucson High, then ducked below Broadway on Park. The mailbox shop that O'Mara found with his license plate trace was only a couple of minutes away. At East 12th Street, I pulled to the curb and looked around. A white Camry was parked in front of a low cinderblock building that took up most of the block. I rolled forward and checked the Camry's rear license plate. It was my shadow's car.

The building had three entrances, apparently for separate businesses. One door's sign said CUSTOMS BROKER. The next had a logo that I recognized as a local payroll services outfit. The third door had no sign at all.

I walked in without knocking. The room was almost bare. A file cabinet sat in a corner. There was a cheap metal desk with a cell phone, a road map, and a manila folder on a blotter, and two office chairs on rollers. Sitting in one of them, with his feet up on the desk, was the tourist in the bad Hawaiian shirt.

"Aloha, Doyle," I said.

He wore the same shirt, this time with faded jeans and tan cowboy boots. The boots looked new and I could smell the leather. His body stayed absolutely still. Only his eyes moved, looking up at me.

"Help you?" he said.

"Yeah," I said. "You can tell me why you're following me around."

"You're mistaken, sir," he said. "I'm just sitting here in my office. You walked in on me. Maybe you're following me around." The midwestern tourist twang that I noticed outside Hector's restaurant had vanished from Doyle's voice.

"Your man in the white Camry was staking out my house," I said. "There's a white Camry outside this building."

"One of the best-selling cars in America, isn't it?" the man called Doyle said. "There might be more than one in Tucson."

"Not with the same license plate," I said.

"Well," he said, "that sure is a coincidence. Will there be anything else?"

I grabbed the other office chair, pulled it up beside him, and sat down. I took out my gun and pointed it at his head. His eyes followed it, but his body remained motionless, at ease, with his feet still propped on the desk.

"A young woman got murdered," I said. "I start looking into it, and you start tailing me here and in Mexico. What's going on?" I moved the gun closer to his head.

"Oh, please," he said. "I'm not some scared kid on a stakeout. You wouldn't have shot his fingers off and you sure as hell won't kill me. Let me give you some advice, Brinker."

"I don't need advice from you," I said.

"Yeah, you do," he said. "You think you know your way around the border 'cause you were on the Patrol and you speak Spanish and you've got a bunch of beaner friends. But it's Chinatown, Jake, you know what I mean? You're going up against a big stone wall."

I stood up, keeping the gun pointed at him. "Stay off my back," I said.

"It's a free country," he said. "I go where I want. You don't like it, shoot me."

I backed out of the office and put away the gun.

I DROVE DOWN THE STREET, DUCKED INTO A PARKING AREA FOR THE drug treatment center at the end of the block, and watched Doyle's building. From my car, I called O'Mara, told him about the office, and gave him the address.

"I'll check it," he said. "But I can tell you right now what we'll get. Phony name on a month-to-month lease for cash. Little businesses move in and out of those blocks all the time. Some are totally honest, some are scammers. He have a phone in there?"

"Just a cell phone," I said. "One less way to find out something about him."

"Typical," O'Mara said. "What do you suppose was in the file cabinet?"

"Good idea," I said.

THE SCARED KID FROM THE STAKEOUT WALKED UP TO DOYLE'S building. He carried a bag from the Carl's Jr. around the corner. Nothing like a couple of breakfast burritos to fortify the team for a hard day of tailing and intimidation.

Twenty minutes later, both men came out. Doyle pulled the door shut but did not lock it with a key. The kid carried the crumpled-up fast-food bag. Doyle carried a canvas attaché case. He swung it lightly from his hand, so I didn't think it had a laptop computer inside. They got into the Camry. The kid drove.

They headed down Park and turned right on 22nd Street, going toward the I-19. That probably meant Mexico. Or they could be heading to Green Valley for a round of golf. I was trying to decide whether or not to follow them when a black Chevy Suburban moved into the left lane to pass me. I looked over and Hector's man Vicente gave me a salute. He pointed to himself, then to the Camry ahead, and stepped on the gas.

I turned around and drove to Doyle's office. The door was unlocked. I went straight to the file cabinet. It had three drawers. All three were empty. On the desk, Doyle had left the manila folder that I had noticed before. One word was written on the tab: LENNOX. Whoever these guys were, they apparently had kept a file on April. But whatever had been in it was gone.

CHAPTER 18

THE NEXT MORNING, I FOUND MY COPY OF THE PHONE MESSAGE LEFT for April at Southwest News Consortium. I dialed the number in Hermosillo.

"*Bueno,*" a woman's voice said. Many Spanish speakers in our part of the world answer the telephone with that word, even if the call is not expected to be good news.

I went with my friendliest tone of voice.

"*¿Señora Esposito?*" I asked. Esposito was the name that Hector had matched to the phone number.

"*Sí.*"

"My name is Brinker," I told her in Spanish. "I'm calling from Tucson."

She said nothing.

"I am a private investigator. I am investigating the death of your nephew," I said.

"I cannot speak to you," she said. The line went silent.

When I was sure that she had disconnected, I dialed her number again. Someone picked up the phone, but there was no *"Bueno"* this time.

"The American reporter who was murdered in Nogales," I said. "That was the woman your nephew called. You yourself called her when he disappeared. I'm certain that she died because she was trying to help your nephew. Now we have to help her, *señora,* or she and your nephew will have died for nothing."

Again she made no sound.

"Please," I said.

"Lo siento, señor," she said in a soft, sad voice. *"Sinceramente."* I am sorry. Truly.

She hung up. I knew that if I dialed again, she would not answer.

ANNA AVILA HAD FINISHED AN ADMINISTRATORS' MEETING AT THE Board of Education. She suggested meeting for a cup of coffee at a cafe on University Boulevard. I drove there, watching my back. Nobody tailed me. I scanned following traffic for the white Camry. I looked in every nearby car for Doyle or the kid. I even checked for Vicente's sleek Suburban. Nothing.

Anna was waiting at a patio table when I arrived. I did a double-take. Sometimes, when shadows fell across her face from the side, she looked just like Dolores. We ordered coffees. Anna had an apple Danish.

"I used to figure that you'd be my brother-in-law, coming over to the house all the time," she said. "Now I have to call you for a date."

"Sorry to let you down," I said.

"The thing is," Anna said, "I feel as though I need to tell you this, so you're sure. Even if you and Dolores never get back together, you're still part of my family. Even if you and Al weren't like brothers, the girls would die if you didn't come around. And I'd be pretty grouchy about it, too."

I reached across the table and touched her hand. "I knew," I said, "but I'm glad you told me."

"So come around, okay?"

"Okay."

She smiled and said, "How's the case?"

I explained where things stood, finishing with my calls to Señora Esposito.

"Who can blame her?" Anna said. "For all she knows, you're one of the bad guys, checking up on her. One wrong word and something nasty happens."

"She'd rather leave her nephew's body unclaimed than identify him," I said. "She cared about him, but now she can't touch him. She's been threatened. That means Juan Doe's identity throws light where it's not wanted. If we learn who he was, then we'll know what he was doing."

"You think it's something to do with the *maquiladoras?*" Anna said.

"It's the only thing that's come up," I said. "Juan Doe said he wanted to talk to April Lennox about oppression and murder. That covers a lot of ground in Mexico, but the oppression part would fit with factories. Some kind of labor beef. And Calderón at the consulate said the murdered Nogales women either worked in the *maquilas* or had connections there, whatever that means."

We sipped our coffee and watched the cheerful college crowd.

"Tuition went up a thousand dollars this year," Anna said. "Lord knows what it will be when Anita and Alicia start."

"They're smart," I said. "They'll get scholarships."

"I hope," she said. She worked on the Danish for a moment, then said, "That girl. April. Was she special to you?"

"She was a good person, I think," I said. "She was a little too earnest in that youthful, lefty way. Save the world from greedy fascists, that kind of thing. But she was nice. She was funny sometimes. She had some demons that I'll probably never learn about. Anyway, she sure as hell didn't deserve what happened to her."

"You mean," Anna said, "she deserved better from you."

"She did," I said. "But it's more than that. She went down there on her own, and she's still alone. The Mexican police want to forget about it. TPD can't do anything unless we connect her murder to the guy who got killed at the basketball riot. Her own father is numb or in shock, or maybe he just doesn't give a damn."

"Some parents don't," Anna said. "Hard to believe, but I've seen it."

"More likely numb," I said. "Dolores told me about a chart in some newsroom where she worked. It was kind of a grid to show why certain stories are important to people. The up-and-down line was things that could happen, like fires and economic change, things like that. The worst thing was a death. That was at the top of the grid. And the left-to-right line was for proximity. If the event happened to somebody you don't know in a faraway place, it was low importance, on the left. But if somebody close was involved, that was high, so it was on the far right."

"You need a chart to know that?" Anna said.

"It was just a way to think about stories," I said. "The most important thing was your own child. So you'd go up the chart for the event, then over to the right for the proximity. The thing at the top right corner was the biggest story, the worst thing that could happen to anyone. That was the death of your child."

"That's sick," Anna said. "Putting an algebraic value on devastation. A grief grid."

"But it's true, isn't it? Now, imagine that your child dies, and nobody will try to find out what happened. That's off the chart."

"But," Anna said, "you're trying."

"Yeah." I took out the business card that Calderón gave me. Carl Brooks, a *maquiladora* manager for Amistadt Enterprises. The card showed a Nogales, Sonora, phone number and another for Green Valley, Arizona.

"I need to talk to this guy," I said.

"Go to Green Valley if you can," Anna said. "Old folks aren't violent. I'll be right back, Brink. Use your cell and call him while I'm gone."

Green Valley, south of Tucson, was known for its planned retirement communities. Some subdivisions there ban children and even young spouses. But other neighborhoods imposed no restrictions. People of all ages lived in and around GV. Many of them had personal or business connections to Mexico, a fast forty miles down Interstate 19.

The woman who answered the phone at Amistadt Enterprises said that Brooks was working in Sonora almost every day. If I wanted to come down to Nogales, he could see me at the *maquiladora* on Friday afternoon at three-thirty.

Anna came back to the table. I told her about the appointment.

"Be careful," she said.

"Broad daylight in the middle of town," I said. "What could go wrong?"

"That's what April Lennox thought," she said.

CHAPTER 19

GABRIELA CORONA PICKED ME UP AT LAX. WHEN I WALKED OUT OF the concourse, she gave me a businesslike hug and said, "'Walking My Cat Named Dog.'"

"No clue," I said.

She laughed. "Norma Tanega, 1966."

"Deeply obscure," I told her.

"Yeah, that was about it for Norma," she said. "But I finally got you, Brinker. You're buying me a long lunch at some classy seaside joint."

"I'd do that anyway," I said. "You're getting me in to see Dickie Ungerlieder, and you're saving me a rental car. But you have to have me back for the four-thirty-five flight."

"There's one at seven-ten," she said. Then, with a sly smile, "Or eight in the morning."

"Now, Gabi," I said. "If I spent the night, you'd have nothing more to look forward to."

"Story of my life," she said. "Our Lady of Perpetual Anticipation."

We picked up her car in the parking garage and headed north on Lincoln Boulevard, Route 1. When we hit the Coast Highway at Santa Monica, the sun was high, and the ocean sparkled even beneath the thin coastal haze. We had the windows down. The sea breeze filled the car with salty air and ruffled Gabi's short black hair. She seemed to be smiling from her toes up.

"I love L.A.," she said.

"Randy Newman," I said.

"No, I mean I really do love L.A. The traffic sucks and the smog can be sickening. But you hit a day like this, cruising along the beach, it's perfect. You ought to move over here, *mijo*. I guarantee you, there's life after Tucson."

"What did you find out about Dickie Ungerlieder?"

"Oh, yeah," she said. "The real purpose of your visit. Well, Dickie's one of the things I *don't* love about L.A. There's a big steaming pile of guys like him over here."

"Meaning?"

"Meaning, he's a creep. He's got a sheet with two disorderlies. Both domestic incidents, as the cops say. He got fines on both, no time served. Had one Percodan possession beef, pleaded down to improper container. A fine, no time. So what we have here is your basic rich druggie who beats up his girlfriends."

"And has lawyers who get him a pass," I said.

"Exactly," Gabi said. "Anyway, we get into his house today because of lucky timing. Dickie is drumming up publicity for a little investment scheme. He wants to build an artists' colony up in Ventura. A place where the brightest lights of film, television, and the lesser creative arts can own homes and share visions of future creativity."

"The lesser creative arts?"

"Books, painting, sculpture, dance. It's L.A., Brinker."

"So he's building a Green Valley for movie and TV people?"

"What I think," Gabi said, "is that he wants to get money to build a bunch of tract houses. He'll sell a couple to former actors on *The Love Boat* or to Jerry Springer, maybe. Then he'll market it to the rubes as a neighborhood of stars."

We came into Malibu. Brown, dry hillsides rose to our right. A few apartment buildings perched precariously there.

"Looks like a dangerous place to live," I said.

"It is," Gabi said. "If the brush fires don't get them, the mudslides will. But, hey, it's Malibu."

To the left, the rich and famous packed themselves along the shore. The small homes looked cheap from the street, but out back, they had that billion-dollar beach.

Dickie Ungerlieder's house seemed narrower than his neighbors' places. A one-car garage opened to the street. A gleaming Jaguar XKR convertible with a new paper license plate sat inside. Gabi pulled her compact sedan into the narrow strip between the busy highway and the houses, blocking Dickie's Jag. We got out and walked a few steps to a white wooden gate. I pushed a button and a man's voice crackled over an intercom. Gabi announced us. A buzzer sounded and the gate popped open.

The grubby roadside feel vanished as we walked down the

narrow path between Dickie's place and the house next door. The ocean lay ahead. The roar of Coast Highway traffic gave way to ocean sounds, little waves breaking and gulls scouting the beach-front terrace tables.

Dickie Ungerlieder wore tight, faded blue jeans and a red pullover sweater. He was short and slender, but with some muscle. He wore his unnaturally brown hair long and combed straight back from a low forehead. He greeted us with a ready smile and jumpy eyes that calculated our net worth before we said a word.

"You're Gabriela," he said, taking her extended hand in both of his. Very good, Dickie, I thought. It had to be one of us.

"And this is Brinker," Gabi said. "He's coming over from our Tucson bureau. A few of us on the metro desk are showing him around the big city."

Dickie gave me a hearty handshake. "From the barren desert to La-La Land," he said. "Good move. You guys want a Bloody Mary?"

"I'd love one," Gabi said, "but we can't while we're working."

"Strictly business, eh?" Dickie said. "Fair enough. How about some fresh orange juice?"

"That sounds great," Gabi said.

"Good. Go on out front, have a seat," Dickie said. "I'll be right with you."

In back, facing the beach, the house was split level. Dickie walked up a half flight to a kitchen. We walked down a few steps to a living room. Sliding glass doors were open to the ocean.

Gabi looked at the view for a moment and said, "I think I could be talked into marrying for money."

"You'd earn every dime," I said. She shrugged.

Dickie came in with two big glasses of orange juice and a Bloody Mary on a tray. He gave us our drinks and pointed us to a big sofa facing the water.

"Have a seat," he said, still with the friendly smile. "Metro, huh? I'd have thought the business desk, or maybe Ventura County bureau for this story."

"I would have, too," Gabi said. "Business is up to their ears in that downtown redevelopment flap, and Ventura's shorthanded because Joe Billings moved to the *Washington Post.*"

"That's right," Dickie said. "I was going to call him, but I heard that he left. Why would he leave here for that? What's in Washington, for chrissakes?"

Gabi had her reporter's notebook out. "Tell me about your project," she said.

Dickie launched his pitch. He even had artist renderings of the retirement community. Happy little stick figures strolled on hiking trails with the Pacific glistening beyond. The woodsy area was dotted with elegant-looking, energy-efficient homes. At the center was a small theater suitable for film screenings and modest plays.

"Brainy stuff. None of that overproduced Broadway crap," he said. "They could have, like, intellectual discussions afterward."

"Wonderful," Gabi said, scribbling away. "What's the expected price range?"

"We don't want it to be snooty," Dickie said. "Nothing over two million."

"You know, Mr. Ungerlieder," I said, "I keep trying to place your name. Have you ever been to Tucson?"

"Had a friend in rehab there," he said. "Pretty good program, if you ever need one." He was looking at me differently, wondering what kind of question that was.

"Somebody mentioned your name to me," I said.

"Julia Roberts, probably," he said. "She's hot for me."

I gave him the laugh he wanted and said, "No, I've got it. It was Jon Cartwright. The reporter from Southwest News Consortium. I met him in Phoenix and said something about wanting to see Malibu when I came to L.A. He said, yeah, Dickie Ungerlieder lives there."

He took a long drink of his Bloody Mary, watching me over the top of the glass.

"He didn't mention Streisand or Geffen, anybody like that living around here? They usually get more attention than I do."

"Just you," I said. "I guess he knows you."

"He doesn't know shit," Dickie said. "Why do I think I'm getting jerked around here?"

"Jerked around?" I said.

"Cartwright is one sneaky son of a bitch," Dickie said. "I know firsthand because he dated a woman I knew. She used to call me and say he beat her up and she had to get away from him."

He stood and walked to the open glass doors. Gabi and I said nothing. Dickie took a deep breath of the salt air, then turned around.

"That prick told you the same thing about me, didn't he?"

"Ever been to Mexico, Dickie?"

"Why? Anything I want from Mexico, I can import." His eyes were moving fast now, blinking and looking from me to Gabi and back to me.

"Did you beat up April Lennox?"

"You'll never know, will you? Can't exactly ask her."

"I asked you."

"Well, guess what, buddy?" he said. "You got no right to ask me anything. April got killed and I'd suspect Cartwright just as much as some Mexican sex fiend. Get outta here, both of you."

Gabi and I stood and started for the door. Dickie said, "I don't suppose I'll be seeing anything about my project in the paper."

"Maybe in the *Onion*," Gabi said.

CHAPTER 20

WE DROVE ALONG THE PCH TO A PLACE CALLED GEOFFREY'S. WE sat outside, on a bluff above the Pacific, in the soft California sunshine. Gabi ordered a bottle of Chalk Hill chardonnay.

"Who's driving?" I said.

"If we eat a lot," she said, "we'll stay under the legal limit."

"What did you think of Dickie?" I asked.

"Pretty much as advertised," she said. "I see how he could simulate charm until you push his buttons."

"Do you know Jon Cartwright?"

"I've run into him on stories. Talked a bit."

"Who's your money on," I said, "for beating up women?"

"Dickie," she said. "Win, place, and show."

"You have good radar for men?"

She leaned in a little closer and smiled. "Are we changing the subject now?"

"Come on, Gabi," I said.

"Well, since you ask," she said, "my radar for men is pathetic. But Dickie's no problem, with his tight little jeans and dyed hair and those wired eyes. I think he's got enough coke in the bedroom to keep a steady traffic of wannabe actresses and nymphets passing through his cool beach pad. And I think he'd bash any woman who didn't kiss his ass. As long as she's smaller than he is."

"Hard to find any people shorter than Dickie," I said.

"They got no reason to live," she said, laughing. "I know, it's Randy Newman again."

The waiter brought the wine. Gabi said to him, "I'm tasting it, but give my date here the bill." She sipped the wine and sighed and smiled at the waiter. He filled our glasses.

"Look at this, Brinker," Gabi said. She clinked glasses with me and swept her free hand to the horizon. "I never thought I'd leave Tucson. All my whole family history's there, just like yours. When I got the L.A. offer, I had dinner with Mama and Papa. I practically cried and told them I didn't want to leave."

She pulled her chair closer to the table. "Papa said, 'If your grandparents didn't want to do better for themselves and for us, they never would have come up to this country. If your mother and I didn't want to do better, I wouldn't have worked two jobs and saved to buy this house.' I'm still crying, and Mama says, 'It's only an hour away.' I said, 'Mama, you'd ride an airplane for me?' She's always been too scared to go on an airplane. She said, 'I'll talk to the pilot and make him promise not to go too fast.'"

Gabi used the crisp linen napkin to wipe her eyes.

"It's a great story," I said.

She smiled and snuffled and said, "The point is, you go for it. You move on. Move up."

I held up the menu and said, "What looks good?"

She stared at me and shook her head.

GABI HAD A SHRIMP SALAD AND I ATE HALIBUT. EVERYTHING WAS perfect. The soft seaside air felt otherworldly wonderful to me. The lunch crowd thinned out and the sun headed down toward Hawaii.

"Back at Dickie's," I said, "you had to be breaking some ethical rules. Telling him you were doing a story when you weren't. Calling me a reporter."

"Maybe I will do a story on him sometime," she said. "I could rationalize it all kinds of ways. I just decided to do it."

"I'm grateful, Gabi."

"If we had another bottle of wine, we'd have to call a cab," she said.

"And the airline probably wouldn't allow a drunk on board," I said.

"If we had another bottle of wine," she said, "you wouldn't be going to the airport."

"Got to," I said. "I have an appointment in Nogales tomorrow."

"I know, I know." She sat back and twirled the stem of her wine glass. She watched a young, impossibly attractive couple walk into the bar. I thought the man was on some cop show, but I couldn't remember which one.

Gabi said, "I'm trying to think of something I can do to help you with this."

"You've done a lot today. Dickie's nasty streak is worth thinking about. I never would have gotten next to him without your help."

"How about if I make amends with him?"

"Gabi, don't be crazy," I said. "We're already on his list. If you suddenly come around, looking friendly, his hustler radar goes on Defcon Five."

"Just a thought," she said. "Glad you're alarmed."

"I have two things to do in Mexico," I said. "First is this *maquila* guy tomorrow. Then I have to see Mrs. Esposito in Hermosillo. If her nephew wasn't connected to the *maquilas* or to April Lennox, then I'm going to see what else I can find out about Dickie."

"Maybe I can get a head start for you," she said.

"Don't go near him, Gabi," I said. "Please."

"Okay. I've got news search services. And some friends may know about him and April."

I looked at my watch.

"Stay," she said.

"Maurice Williams and the Zodiacs, 1960," I said.

"Yeah," she said. "But that's not what I meant."

I HAD BEEN HOME ABOUT AN HOUR WHEN GABI CALLED.

"Just wanted to be sure you made it," she said. "And I have some news."

"I slept off the Chardonnay on the plane," I said. "What's up?"

"As soon as I get home," she said, "the phone rings. I'm unlisted. Guess who got my number?"

"Don't say Dickie."

"Dickie," she said.

"What did he want?"

"To make up, or so he claimed. He said he wanted to apologize for being a jerk. Listen to this. He says that he just got upset when he thought about poor April. Anyway, he wants to prove to me that he's not a bad guy. He said he'll take me to Chinois on Main for dinner tomorrow night."

"What did he say when you turned him down?" I asked.

She didn't answer.

"Don't do it, Gabi. Stay clear of that guy. He's trouble. You said it yourself."

"He may be good for some more information about April. I told him I'd meet him at the restaurant. He doesn't come to my place. No way. I'm never alone with him."

"I still don't like it," I said.

"Brinker, he's not going to murder me in Chinois on Main. They'd never give him a good table again."

"Gabi, it's not funny. Somebody grabbed April Lennox from the front door of the busiest hotel in Hermosillo."

"Hermosillo's not Santa Monica, Brink. And she didn't know who to look out for. I do. Besides, if Dickie wanted to jam me up, all he had to do was call my editor. I'd probably get fired for our little stunt today."

"I'm worried about this," I said.

"You're going to Mexico tomorrow," she said. "Worry about yourself."

CHAPTER 21

LUIS DONALDO COLOSIO SHOULD HAVE BEEN ELECTED PRESIDENT OF Mexico in 1994. He was the chosen candidate of the Institutional Revolutionary Party, known as PRI. His party held Mexican politics in a death grip for most of the twentieth century. Colosio, though, was widely expected to break the pernicious government traditions of repression and kleptocracy. He was assassinated as he campaigned in the streets of Tijuana. A killer was convicted, but millions of Mexicans believed that corrupt PRI leaders, fearing reform, had engineered the murder of their own guy.

Today, Boulevard Luis Donaldo Colosio connects many of the Nogales *maquiladoras* to the Mariposa Port of Entry, the freight customs station at the Arizona border. Two miles east, most noncommercial traffic moves through the fence at a checkpoint for tourist pedestrians and automobiles. I used that one again, walking along

Avenida Obregón past the bars and discount dentists and *farmacias*. I passed the consulate and soon reached Amistadt Enterprises.

"Let me guess," Carl Brooks said. "You were expecting a sweatshop. Sad-eyed, hungry little kids chained to lathes, right?"

I had to laugh. We were standing in his office, a balcony-level captain's bridge with glass walls and a view of the sprawling production floor in Building One.

"Not that bad," I said. "Maybe a big nasty overseer walking up and down with a whip."

"That would be me." He smiled, not at all offended. "Everybody thinks that about the *maquilas,*" he said. "All the do-gooders bitch and moan and get on the news. But you don't see anybody down there complaining."

This building made electronic circuit boards. Employees sat at tidy workstations, soldering, testing, boxing up the product. The assembly line was immaculate. The employees looked cool and comfortable in their company T-shirts or street clothes. Big air-conditioning ducts poured cool air into the work area. Most of the people on the floor were young, in their late teens and twenties. The women laughed and shouted across the rows to each other. The men were more quiet, except for a few flirts. They were obvious even to me in the quiet office above. But everyone kept their hands moving, their eyes on the work, the boxes steadily sliding onto the conveyer belt. I flashed on Lucy and Ethel at the chocolate factory, but no such chaos ruled here. The work rolled on, steady and competent.

"Have a seat," Brooks said.

He worked at a big, practical steel desk. The photographs on the wall behind him showed a successful middle manager: arms around smiling employees on the shop floor, sitting at a large mahogany table with several Mexican men in dark suits, a ribbon-cutting with a diverse, well-groomed group identified as the board of directors. Lousy picture, I thought. Half of the directors were standing in a shadow from the building. A small caption identified everyone, though. A big headline read, *"Amistadt: Global y local."* Beside the photographs was an Arkansas Razorbacks football pennant.

"Amistadt is an international investment firm," he said. "You know the word Spanish word *amistad,* for friendship. We added the 't' to the end because of our German partners. *Stadt* is German for city. So we think of ourselves here as a city of friendship. Global and local."

"Ah," I said.

"I know, I know, it sounds hokey," Brooks said. "But this is the friendship of the new global economy, Mr. Brinker. Solid technology moving freely across borders. Reasonably priced and highly productive workforces. Sensible government policies and cooperation."

"How do those folks down there live on a dollar an hour?" I asked.

Brooks sighed. "Many of our employees make considerably more. But even at entry level, these folks do a hell of a lot better than most of their countrymen, who live on far less. We Americans tend to see these things in our terms. Where's the twenty bucks an hour, the Blue Cross, all that? Well, sure, if this were Chicago or Detroit or even Phoenix. But this is Mexico."

He got up and walked to the window overlooking the shop.

"Those folks down there, almost four thousand total in our companies, they make thirty percent more than people working in Mexican-owned factories in this very town," he said. "That's true at all the *maquilas,* Amistadt's and other companies' places. We have employer-paid cafeterias. We give out the local equivalent of food stamps with many pay envelopes. If somebody needs an advance before payday, we make it happen. I'll give it to them out of my own pocket, if I have to."

He returned to the chair behind his desk. "But you're not here for a lesson on free markets and magnanimous employers, are you?"

"No," I said.

"Well, fire away," he said. "We're pretty much an open book around here."

"Do you have any idea," I said, "why so many of the women murdered here in Nogales were *maquila* workers? Any possible connection to the job?"

"Oh, boy," he said. "I used to tell people that we've been accused of everything but murder. Now I can't even say that."

"I don't mean the company did anything wrong," I said. "Do you know of anything happening with those women here? Any problems or disputes? Any shop-floor talk about stalkers?"

"Let's be clear about something, Mr. Brinker," he said. "Only three of those poor women worked at Amistadt facilities, and one of them was a former employee. So my knowledge of the big picture is limited."

"Okay," I said.

"As for those who worked here, we had no problems. We heard of no problems. The one former employee had quit to go take care of her sick mother in southern Mexico someplace. That happens all the time at the *maquilas*. She came back to town and went to work someplace else. That's common, too."

"And you didn't hear any personal stories about any of them?"

"No, but I wouldn't have. I go home at night to Green Valley. I spend all my free time with my wife and our two children." He turned around a framed photograph on his desk. They were posed in front of a red SUV parked on the driveway of a large home by a golf course.

"Nice-looking family," I said.

"Thank you," Brooks said. "But these folks here in Nogales have a different life. A lot of them are single. On Friday night, they take their pay and head downtown to the discos and bars. Obviously there's drinking. There's probably drug use. Lord knows what sort of strange characters hang around to prey on young women. They don't have to be *maquila* workers, or in Mexico, to face that kind of danger."

I looked at the pictures of Brooks with his smiling employees. For a dollar an hour, they did seem to be a surprisingly cheery family.

"Any labor troubles here?" I asked.

Brooks smiled. "We've never had so much as a grievance," he said, "let alone a job action of any kind. It's a happy shop."

"Or a docile union," I said.

"Well, Mr. Brinker, I'm in business, so I try to be a realist," he said. "I take happiness however I can."

"Me, too," I said. "Can I talk to some of your employees?"

"Not while they're working," he said. "But on their own time, well, it's a free country."

CHAPTER 22

VICENTE WAITED ACROSS THE STREET, STANDING IN THE SHADE OF A *mini super* awning, drinking from a small carton of orange juice. I walked over. A poster advertising a bullfight was in the corner of the little store's front window.

"He confess?" Vicente said.

"Breaking down fast," I said, laughing. "You have a crush on me or what?"

He did not look amused. "Boss said to keep an eye on you, just in case the bad guys stay on your tail."

"Thanks," I said.

"He didn't let you talk to any employees, did he?" Vicente said.

"Just his own genial self," I said. "I think I missed something with him, but I can't figure out what it was."

"Imagine that," Vicente said. "Anyway, in a couple of hours, it'll be Friday night. You want to take the Nogales nightlife tour? Up close and personal. See how the wild and crazy young *maquila* workers live and love when they cash those paychecks."

"On a dollar an hour," I said.

"Yeah, well," he said, "girls get discounts when they party."

We went to Hector's restaurant for an early dinner. Tourists crowded the dining room. As we walked to our table, I heard one diner say, "You can get this at Taco Bell for seventy-nine cents. Shouldn't it be cheaper down here?" The waiter rolled his eyes as we walked by. Vicente pointed a finger, pistol-style, at the back of the tourist's head.

Vicente apparently had a standing order in the kitchen. A waiter produced a tequila bottle as soon as we sat down. Vicente poured two small glasses and pushed one to me.

"Salad, amor y pesetas," he said, downing the shot. Health, love, and money. *Pesetas* were the pre-Euro currency of Spain. Maybe Mexicans know that wishing for *pesos* does little good.

"Y el tiempo para gustarlos," I said, finishing the traditional toast. And the time to enjoy them.

"Yeah, that, too," Vicente said. "My line of work, though, I don't always think about a long time."

"Go straight," I said.

"Chicano high school dropout with only one job, and I can't put it on a résumé," he said. "I'd be a hot property on the job market."

Three tables away, a tourist shouted, "Can we drink this water?"

"Let's kill 'em all," Vicente said. "We got some major weaponry back in the boss's office."

"Even the innocent bystanders?" I said, pretty sure he was kidding.

"Let the locals go," he said. "They won't see anything."

NIGHT FELL AND THE YOUNG CROWDS GATHERED AT EL PÁJARO Rojo. The red neon parrot's gold eye winked as we walked in. The bouncer pointed to a sign that read LOS EMPLEADOS DE LAS MAQUILADORAS: ENTRADA LIBRE. Apparently I didn't look like a Nogales factory employee, so he wanted the cover charge. Vicente came up behind me and nodded to the man. The bouncer nodded back and pushed the swinging door aside. We walked through to the bar.

"*Obreros,* the *maquila* workers, get in free with their ID cards on payday," Vicente said. "Attracts a bunch of babes, and that brings in the men."

It worked for everybody on this night. The dance floor vibrated with sweaty couples bouncing to deafening salsa rap and other sounds that probably had names I didn't know. Beer came in buckets, six or seven bottles packed down in ice. Many of the women drank colorful Waikiki-wannabe cocktails with red parrot swizzle sticks.

Vicente and I leaned against the bar and ordered Dos Equis.

"I feel old," I said. "These kids will think we're cops."

"No," Vicente said. "If it's only me, maybe. But you don't look like a Nogales cop. Just because you hang around with Mexicans back home don't make you a Mexican down here, Brinker."

As if on cue, two young women sauntered over. Their white jeans, in a thin shiny material, might have been sprayed on. One wore a pink wool sweater about a size too small. The other showed a minimal bra through a filmy white blouse. They sported big happy smiles and walked with a wiggly bounce in their step.

"How you doing?" the sweater girl said. It sounded like "Ow you dween?" but the cadence was easy and I figured they would speak English.

"Not bad," I said. Vicente just nodded.

"Not even a little bad?" she said. Both women laughed.

"What's your names?" Vicente asked.

"I am Frida," the one in the tight sweater said. "Like in the movie."

"I am María," the other said. "Like in the Bible."

They both laughed again. Even Vicente cracked a smile.

"What is yours?" Frida asked.

"Vicente."

"Like *el presidente,*" Frida said. The president of Mexico was named Vicente Fox. Frida looked to me.

"Brinker," I said.

"I don't know what that is like," she said. "You boys are from Arizona? Scottsdale, maybe?" Hope springs eternal.

"I'm a citizen of the world," Vicente said.

"Ooh," María said. "International man of mystery."

"You ladies work at the *maquilas*?" I said.

"Sure. Everybody works there," María said, wiggling a little closer to me. "You guys want to buy us a drink?"

"Our pleasure," Vicente said. "What would you like?"

"I want a Slippery Nipple," Frida said.

"Sure you do, but what do want to drink?" Vicente said.

Frida and María thought that was hilarious. María was still

laughing when she said, "Slow Comfortable Screw for me. That's what I want to drink, okay?"

"You guys order the drinks while we go pee," Frida said. "Don't go away."

"We'll be right here," Vicente said. The women walked, arm in arm, to the rest rooms at the other end of the bar.

"They're going to work it out," Vicente said. "Who takes who. What they should get out of it."

"One more drink order like that," I said, "and I'm asking the deejay for ABBA."

"Yeah, they're a little behind on the fads," Vicente said. "Those accents sound pretty far south. They probably just came up here for work. They could be Guatemalans, for all I know."

"They said they work at the *maquilas*. Are they hookers, too?" I said.

Vicente was looking around the room, taking in the crowd, the way a bodyguard does. "Nah," he said. "There's some in here, I suppose. A few of them'll blow you for a beer. But mostly it's just *maquila* girls wanna have fun and save their money. You buy a few drinks, connect, everybody has a good time, *no problemas*."

"Is this a great country, or what?" I said.

"You're not getting out enough at home, son," Vicente said. "They've got yuppie joints pretty much like this in Tucson. Just higher prices, and nobody's ordered those stupid drinks for years."

Frida and María had found a table and waved to us. Vicente paid the bartender. We took the drinks and pushed our way through the crowd. The deejay spun something with enough bass and volume to threaten the structural integrity of the building.

"So where do you beauties live?" Vicente said.

"We share an apartment," María said. "Is close to work. We are lucky we found a good place."

"Beats the *colonias,* eh?" Vicente said. Many *maquiladora* workers lived in densely packed neighborhoods of hillside shacks without running water or electricity.

"Sure," Frida said. "I went shopping once in Tucson. They had this big store for, how do you say, *mascotas.*"

"Pets," I said.

"Yes, pet animals," she said. "And they had houses for dogs there. To sell to people, you know? And some of those houses were better than the ones in the *colonias.*"

"So how can you afford that nice apartment?" Vicente said.

"People do things for each other," Frida said. She and María laughed, but without much humor.

"Tough town," I said.

"Is not bad," María said. "Where we come from, the houses are awful, too, but there is no work."

"Your jobs are good?" I said.

"Sure," Frida said. María said nothing.

"Where do you work?"

"Amistadt Building Number Three," María said. "We make cable TV boxes. I have a friend in Building Four who makes wires for big jet planes."

She saw me wince and said, "No, they are good. If I ever fly in a plane, I hope it has her wires. Very safe. All new computer equipment to make them. And my friend Corazón is a very good worker."

"They treat you right at Amistadt?" I said.

"Sure," Frida said. "We could use more pee breaks. I think the pee break rules were made by a man."

"You should get a union," I said. "A labor union."

"We have a *sindicato*," María said, "but it is, you know, not really for us too much."

"A company union," Vicente said.

The women shrugged. María had her hand on my leg now, and turned so her breasts touched my arm.

"Did you know those girls from the *maquilas* who got murdered?" I asked.

Frida said quickly, "Some of those girls were not from the *maquilas*. They were *putas*. That is a dangerous thing, always."

María said, "I knew one. She worked in my building."

Frida shot her a hard look, but María went on. "Her name was Alma. She was a sweet girl. She was no *puta*. I don't think she ever even, you know, had a boyfriend. There was one guy. He left town after she died."

Vicente and I exchanged an uh-oh glance.

María said, "All the time, Alma wanted to help people. When her friends got sick, Alma would bring them food and feed their babies and do anything they needed. And she always tried to get Señor Brooks to pay us more money and give us more breaks."

Frida said in rapid Spanish, "María, you shouldn't be talking like this with guys we just met. We don't know these guys. It's one thing to have some drinks and go home with them, but talking about work is stupid, girl."

"We're not from the company," I said in Spanish. Frida and María looked surprised.

"Tell you what," Vicente said. "I have a place not far from here. It has the best liquor stock in Nogales and it's private. We can say whatever we like there."

"This is crazy," Frida said.

"I don't care," María said. "These guys are nice."

"Crazy," Frida said again.

Vicente opened his jacket slightly so Frida could see what was under it. She looked and jerked back.

"*Policía* will put you in jail for that," Frida said.

"*Policía* won't bother me," Vicente said. "Frida, you have a big purse. Right now, you can lean up against me, like we're in love. While I embrace you, you take that gun from its holster and put it into your purse. It's real and it's loaded. That puts you in charge of whatever happens from here on. Take it, *querida,* and come with us."

Frida's eyes looked bigger than those kids' eyes in the black velvet paintings at gift shops on Avenida Obregón. She had her hand in Vicente's jacket and her whole arm trembled.

"Just take it by the grip," Vicente said. "Don't touch the trigger, now. I don't want you to shoot me in the heart."

María said, "You have champagne at your place?"

"From France," Vicente said. "Best in the world."

Frida watched his face as she pulled her hand from his jacket. She plunged the object she held into her purse. Vicente's eyes never left hers. He kept smiling. Finally, she did, too.

"Okay," Frida said.

CHAPTER 23

WE WALKED FIVE BLOCKS TO VICENTE'S APARTMENT, LOOKING ORDINARY: two guys who connected with two younger women at El Pájaro Rojo. The apartment was in a three-story building across the street from Hector's restaurant. On the sidewalk, Vicente unlocked an unmarked door. He said to Frida, "Keep your hand out of the purse for a minute."

We entered a small lobby. A man sat in a straight-backed chair with a semiautomatic pistol, a cell phone, and an opened can of Fresca on a wooden table. He was reading a paperback book called *Deuda de Sangre.* He nodded at Vicente and looked carefully at the women and me. We started up a stairwell to the second floor.

Frida looked back at the man and said, "Who was that guy?"

"Concierge," Vicente said.

"What's that?" Frida asked.

"El conserje," Vicente said. "He makes my restaurant reservations, sends out my laundry, things like that."

María giggled and said, "A very dangerous work."

The stairs led to a small landing. Vicente produced two more keys and opened the double-locked apartment door. He stood aside for the women and me. The apartment looked like a standard U.S. rental unit with beige carpet and white walls with mass-produced paintings of desert landscapes. The leather chairs and sofa looked real and new. Frida and María plopped down on the sofa and wiggled around on the novel luxury. Frida kept the big purse in her lap.

"This is nice," María said. "How much is the rent?"

"My boss pays," Vicente said from the adjacent kitchen. We heard a champagne cork pop. "It's a business apartment."

"Ooh," María said. "What business?"

"Export goods," Vicente said. He came back to the living room with four long-stemmed glasses hooked in the fingers of one hand and a bottle of Perrier-Jouët in the other.

"Pretty bottle," María said.

"I knew you'd like it," Vicente said. He poured carefully and passed glasses to each of us. "We have some Dom Perignon, but the bottles don't look as good."

We sipped and murmured approval. Frida and María took long drinks and Vicente refilled their glasses. Frida reached into her purse. Vicente did not move, but I saw him watching her. His posture seemed tighter, ready to spring.

Frida withdrew the gun, holding it by its barrel. She handed it to Vicente.

"Take this thing back," she said. "I don't want to shoot it. If you were going to kill us, you would save the champagne."

Vicente smiled and put the gun back into the holster.

"Tell me more about Alma," I said.

"One night we went out to party," Frida said. "It was a Friday, like tonight. We were at El Pájaro Rojo then, too. Alma left early. She always went home early. María and I stayed late. Then on Monday, Alma did not come to work. Or Tuesday. They found a girl's body on Tuesday near Colonia Escobedo. On Wednesday, they said it was Alma."

"Police said she was probably a *puta* and she went with the wrong guy, you know?" María said. "That was so stupid. Anyone who knew Alma knew that was wrong. I was so mad."

"Why do you think they said that?" I asked. Vicente filled their glasses again and went to the kitchen for another bottle.

"You have some music?" Frida said. "We should dance."

"Because they don't want to hear anything bad about Amistadt," María said. "Señor Brooks always says we need to have a good, eh, *concepto popular*." She looked to see if I understood.

"Public image," I said. "The way the company looks to the public."

"Yes," María said. "Last year, two men in my building got drunk and broke some windows on Avenida Obregón. They got fired the next day."

Frida was dancing by herself without music.

"Tell me about Alma's boyfriend," I said.

"Ricardo Esposito," María said. "He was nice."

"Esposito," I said.

"María," Frida said, stopping her dance, "we are not supposed to talk about this."

"I don't care," María said. She turned to face me. "Yes, Esposito. You know what? He went away two days after we heard that it was Alma who was killed. He did not tell anyone. You know what else? That stinks, because Ricardo would never do that."

"What do you mean?" I asked.

"Ricardo treated Alma with respect," she said. "All the other guys at our building and in the bars, they have no respect for women. They just want to . . . you know."

Frida said, "That's okay sometimes." She winked at Vicente.

"That is us," María said. "We know what we are doing. But Alma was, eh, innocent. Ricardo always treated her like a decent girl. He even treated us like we were decent."

Frida said, "I liked that."

"Did the company say anything about Ricardo's going away?" I asked.

"Señor Brooks said Ricardo was, we say, *desconsolado*?"

"Heartsick," I said.

"Yes, his heart was sick because Alma died. So he quit work and went home."

I asked, "Was his home in Hermosillo?"

"How did you know that?" Frida said.

"What did Ricardo do at work?" I asked.

"Same as me," María said. "He made the boxes for the cable TV."

"I mean, did he do anything besides his job? Something that got him in trouble with the company?"

María reached for the champagne bottle and poured a glass for herself. She started to fill mine, but I put my hand over it.

"Got to drive home," I said.

María looked surprised. "Too bad," she said. "But I tell you what. Ricardo wanted to make things better for us. For all the workers, you know."

"Did the company know?"

"Sure," Frida said. "They know everything."

"Señor Brooks knew," María said. "He told Ricardo to stop or he would get fired. Ricardo told Alma and she told me. But she said she would do what Ricardo wanted. She was going to help him make a better, what did you call the *sindicato*?"

"Labor union," I said.

"Yes," María said. "Ricardo wanted to have a strong union of all the *obreros* in Nogales."

"I asked you once," Frida said. "How did you know Ricardo was from Hermosillo?"

"I think our paths crossed once," I said. "I don't want to say more until I'm sure."

"He's dead, isn't he?" María said. "I knew it. I knew it the day he was gone." I expected her to cry, but she didn't. She spoke with the emotional neutrality of a newscaster reporting death in a faraway place.

IT WAS DAWN WHEN I GOT HOME. THERE WAS NO MESSAGE FROM Gabi, who had promised to call after her dinner with Dickie Ungerlieder.

The pale orange light built behind the Catalinas, then seemed to catch fire as the sun cleared the foothills' horizon.

CHAPTER 24

I SLEPT FOR A COUPLE OF HOURS, THEN TRIED TO CALL GABI. SHE DID not answer at home. Her cell number asked callers to leave voice mail. The metro desk at the paper didn't expect her in on the weekend.

It was Saturday morning. Traffic was heavy as I headed down Oracle, past the shopping mall and the auto mall. Downtown Tucson was deserted. The sad, shabby *centro* had no reason to exist when government offices were closed.

I let myself into the Alejandro & Katz building. Two young associates were hunched over law books and legal tablets in their tiny offices. We were the only people there.

I checked my mail and threw most of it straight into the trash. I called both of Gabi's numbers and struck out. I walked to the front desk and looked over Lupita's message book from the last several days. Nothing for me.

The office had a small canteen room with a coffeemaker. I asked the young lawyers if they wanted some. They had the sleep-starved look of all the newbies, so I was not surprised when they said yes. I made a big pot and took cups to them.

Coffee failed to clear my head. I went outside and walked south to Congress, past the new federal courthouse, and back to Alejandro & Katz. Two ideas rattled around in my head. Something from Brooks's office at the *maquila,* and something Jon Cartwright had said. Did the two fit together somehow?

When I heard my cell phone, I punched the talk button before the second ring and yelled, "Hello?"

Gabriela Corona said, "I'm alive."

"God, Gabi, I wondered."

"Spent the night with Dickie Ungerlieder, and lived to tell the tale."

I felt myself taking a breath. The depth of my feeling surprised me.

"Spent the night?" I said.

"Oh, please," Gabi said. "It was more like spent the evening. Hey, that's kind of touching, Brinker. Who knew?"

"What happened?"

"Dickie shows up, all sweetness and light. Had a coat and tie, even. He was downright pleasant through dinner. Good talker. Good listener, for short stretches. Spared no expense on the dinner, too."

"Then what?"

"Then we went out to get our cars. He asked me if I wanted to go back to Malibu for a while. I said thanks, but I have a big day coming up. The usual dodge. He's got his hand on my arm and he starts squeezing it, saying I really need to go home with him. He keeps squeezing and getting that nasty look of his."

"Did you have any Mace in your purse?"

"I said, Dickie, I bruise easily, and you're leaving the evidence on my arm for a battery complaint. And he let go, and looked at me in the ugliest way, and called me a four-letter word that even I will not repeat."

"Are you okay, Gabi?" I asked her.

"Sure. I watched myself when I went home. Stayed awake quite a while, just in case. You didn't catch me this morning because I was running errands."

My heart slowed down. I figured we got away with one.

"So what do you think about him now?" I said.

"I think if there was no crowd of customers and parking attendants, he would've broken my arm and never given it a second thought. That's one creepy guy, Brink."

"Would he kill someone?"

"Who knows? But if a woman really rubbed him wrong, and did it with nobody to see his reaction, I wouldn't put it past him."

"I'll find a way to deal with him," I said. "You stay clear of him, now."

"You bet," she said. "Anyway, I thought of what I could do for you next."

"YOU'RE KIDDING," I SAID.

She wasn't. "Face it," she said. "I'm perfect for this."

Riding to the airport, I had told her about Mrs. Esposito in Hermosillo.

"You haven't spent much time down there, Gabi," I said. "I know you have perfect Spanish and you can ask the right questions, but this isn't your fight."

"Look," she said, "if you confront Mrs. Esposito, she'll panic and clam up again. What are you to her? Just a big American man snooping around something that scares her to death. But if I go, it softens everything. I'll put on a modest black dress like my mother used to wear. Maybe a shawl, like I just came from mass. She'll think, What a *señorita decente,* a respectable girl. I won't be threatening to her."

"I don't want you risking this," I said.

"You need to get this thing behind you, Brink," she said, "and I have a way to help you. And there could be a great story in it for me if things pan out."

"April Lennox got killed down there, Gabi."

"I'm not saying I'm smarter or tougher than she was," Gabi said. "But she had no way to blend in. She was a California blonde. She was probably bumbling around with a Michelin map and some prep school Spanish class accent. Any idiot could tail her down there. But I look like every other woman in Hermosillo."

"You?" I said. "You look like Miss Mexico."

"Oh, sure, right," she said. "If I lose the L.A. makeup and put on Mama's dress, I can be the plainest Jane in town. And once I'm there, I know how to talk to people and get information."

"They'll be on you from the start," I said. "Whoever the bad guys are, they're like spies. You don't see them. They were watching April the minute she got off the plane."

"They were already watching both of you," she said. "Nobody's watching me. Nobody's looking out for the Los Angeles flight. I breeze in, catch Señora Esposito, we have a nice talk, then I get the evening plane back to L.A."

"What if she's being watched?" I said.

"I don't think she is," Gabi said. "If you're right, whoever is doing this has killed about ten people already. They would have killed her, too."

I stood by the kitchen's east window, watching the sun spill white-orange light through gossamer morning clouds.

"What will you tell her?" I asked.

"What you told me. You have the man's name. We don't have to mention those bimbettes from the *maquila.* We just say that you'll give the name to the Tucson police. No point in her holding back anymore. She can claim his body and bring him home. She can tell me whatever she knows about Ricardo and the *maquilas* and nobody will know it came from her."

"She can say the cops called her with the ID, instead of the other way around," I said.

"Exactly."

"Gabi, it makes sense to me. I wonder if it will to a scared lady in Hermosillo."

"Trust me," she said.

CHAPTER 25

SHE CALLED ME ON SUNDAY MORNING TO SAY SHE WAS HEADING FOR the airport. I told her to be careful and wondered if this was the worst idea anyone ever had.

Vicente picked up his cell phone on the third ring. Two familiar voices laughed in the background.

"It's Brinker," I said. "Sounds like you're still at home."

"The laughter of happy women follows me wherever I go," he said. "But yeah, I'm still here."

"I need to ruin your day," I said.

"Somebody has to," he said. "What?"

I told him what I wanted. He said he could do it personally. It was not something to be farmed out.

"You'd better not take Frida and María," I said.

"You're telling me," he said. "Another day with these two and I'm in the orthopedic hospital."

"Call me," I said. "Early and often."

"Don't worry about it," he said.

I WORRIED ABOUT IT. I MENTALLY TRACKED HER PROGRESS TO THE airport, through security, at the gate. Aeroméxico's Web site had the Hermosillo flight departing on schedule.

Al showed up about the time Gabi would be arriving at LAX. We decided to hike for an hour along the Gates Pass trail, in the mountains west of town, then have the Sunday buffet at La Fuente.

Halfway out to the mountains, Al said, "You've looked at your watch four times already."

"I'm going crazy here," I said. "I shouldn't have let her do this."

"*Let* her?" Al said. "Check your calendar, Brink. It's the twenty-first century."

I looked at my watch again. "What's going to happen with Juan Doe?" I said.

"You give the name and whatever you know to O'Mara tomorrow," he said. "He'll give it to Tomás Puente. It's Puente's case. O'Mara will look good for coming up with the name. Puente can notify the next known kin."

"That'll be Mrs. Esposito."

"Right," Al said. "She's the only relative we know about. Puente may want to go through Hermosillo police or the State Judicial Police in Sonora to notify her."

"I don't like that," I said. "Whoever did this probably has someone on the local forces and SJP."

"They're going to find out anyway," Al said.

"Maybe we could prime the press," I said. "Let out a story that independent investigation developed a lead to the unknown man's identity. We could say it was finally confirmed, and we notified Mrs. Esposito. She was shocked at the news. That would take some heat off her."

"And put it on you," Al said.

"They're already watching me," I said.

We pulled into the Gates Pass parking lot. I checked my watch again.

"Oh, boy," Al said. "This is going to be a long afternoon."

"She's probably getting on the Hermosillo plane about now," I said.

"You ever hear that George Carlin routine about airline announcements?" Al said. "He says, 'What do you mean, get *on* the plane. I want to get *in* the plane.'"

I laughed in spite of worrying about Gabi.

Al said, "He says, 'What do you mean, this flight is *nonstop?*'"

Now we both were laughing. Two earnest hikers in little shorts and big shoes walked by and glared. No laughing permitted in the presence of nature, apparently.

We got out of the car and followed the grumps along the trail, maintaining respectful silence. That was easy, with thousands of great saguaro cacti spread out on the desert floor below. Some of them had lived for two centuries in this broiling climate. They're symbols of Arizona, but a patch of the Sonoran Desert is virtually the only place to find them.

"You don't look too gimpy," Al said.

I had been shot in the hip a couple of years before. It would never be quite right, but moving was easier now. A short, easy hike had become more therapeutic than painful.

"Warm weather and pain pills," I said. "It's a slow mend, but I'm getting there."

Three more hikers walked past us, but this group was all smiles and good-mornings. One guy offered us his bottle of water. Al assured them that we were headed back to the trailhead soon.

"She's got to be taking off from LAX now," I said.

"Update me every thousand feet above sea level," Al said. "I wouldn't want to fall behind on the news."

"Hector's man Vicente drove down to Hermosillo this morning," I said. "He'll watch the airport, then follow her into town and keep an eye on her."

"If you're working with Hector's crew on this," Al said, "I really shouldn't know about it."

"Fair enough, Captain."

We walked for another hundred yards. Al said, "This Vicente, he know what he's doing?"

"He can tail me and the people tailing me at the same time," I said.

Al nodded and walked on. He was ahead of me on the trail, but I thought I saw him smile.

WE LOADED UP OUR FIRST PLATE AT LA FUENTE. I HAD CARNITAS IN A red chile sauce, spinach enchiladas, and chilaquiles. Al took the same plus two tamales. As we returned to our table, my cell phone vibrated. I put the plate of food down and walked quickly to the lobby.

"She landed," Vicente said. "No problem at the airport. I'm behind her taxi now, and there's nobody on us."

"Stay close," I said.

"Relax," he said. The line went dead.

The waitress was at our table, taking drink orders. Al had iced tea. I asked for a shot of Cuervo Gold and a Dos Equis.

"Problems?" Al said.

"She's there," I said. "Vicente's watching."

"Terrific carnitas today," Al said. "They got the chile just right, and the meat's perfect."

"How many times have you and I come here with Anna and Dolores?" I asked.

"Lost track years ago," Al said. "I notice that Dolores isn't the reporter you're worried about today."

"I feel helpless," I said. "Gabi's not even connected to this case. And my only connection to her is a narco hood I met less than a week ago."

Al peeled back the husk from a tamale. He spoke quietly. "The world's upside down. You trust a drug dealer. I take a little girl out of a sewer tunnel and finesse the system to keep her as our own daughter. Does the end justify the means?"

"Those ends did," I said. "Hector saved my life, and Dolores's, too. Alicia would have died in that tunnel, or had a life not worth living."

We ate quietly for a while. The mariachis took the small stage and played the old Mexican tunes. I looked at my watch and ordered another Cuervo Gold. In the background of my consciousness, Al said something about a spring training exhibition game when the UA played the Cleveland Indians. The mariachis went into *"Lejos de ti."* Far from you.

The phone vibrated. This time I answered without leaving the table.

"She's in," Vicente said.

CHAPTER 26

THIS IS WHAT GABI TOLD ME WHEN SHE CALLED FROM LOS ANGELES that night.

She changed her clothes in the rest room at LAX. With her mother's modest black dress, with soft speech and shyly averted eyes, she became for that day a pious young Mexican woman returning to her home.

The plane departed with only half its seats filled. Gabi had a row to herself. Only the flight attendant spoke to her. The attendant smiled and seemed solicitous, but avoided the familiarity that strangers often assumed with Gabi's outgoing personality.

At Hermosillo, the taxi driver leered, but Gabi shamed him with the good girl's don't-even-think-about-it scowl. He did not try to make conversation. He drove her straight to the address on Calle de la República.

The woman who answered Gabi's knock was short and picking up the pounds of middle age. She wore a loose-fitting black dress that might have been Gabi's own, except for the size.

"*¿Señora Esposito?*" Gabi said.

"*Sí,*" the woman answered.

"My name is Gabriela Corona," Gabi said in Spanish. "I have come from California to beg you to talk to me about Ricardo. He has been identified now. No harm will come to you if you speak to me about him."

The woman stared at her, unable to decide what to do.

"Please," Gabi said. "You will help me, and yourself, and Ricardo."

In a moment, Señora Esposito said, "You seem like a decent girl. Come in."

"THE POOR LADY WAS RELIEVED," GABI SAID TO ME. IT WAS ALMOST midnight. I sat at the kitchen table, a beer in one hand and the phone in the other.

"They have a nice little house," Gabi said. "Her husband is a manager of a travel agency. He started as a janitor there, went to some little business school, eventually got an office job, and worked his way up."

"So, they're people who didn't have much," I said. "And now that they have a little comfort, it was scary to see what happened to someone like Ricardo, who pushed too hard."

"Yes," Gabi said. "Mr. Esposito's brother, Ricardo's father, didn't do so well, and died young. That's why Ricardo was still a laborer, and still taking on working people's causes."

"Were the Espositos threatened?" I asked.

"No. But Ricardo told them that if he ever got hurt or worse, they should stay out of it. Not try to help him, or even claim his body if he got killed."

"He thought he might get killed?"

"That's what he told them. Mrs. Esposito was appalled, but her husband seemed reconciled to the situation. He said Ricardo knows what he wants to do. She actually wanted to come forward."

"That's why she called April Lennox."

"Yes, to get her started on bringing all this to light. She knew that Ricardo had tried to meet with April. Then when April got killed, Mr. Esposito said '*no más.*' He was afraid that anybody involved with Ricardo's death would be killed."

I got another beer from the refrigerator. "So was Ricardo in love with a *maquila* worker named Alma?" I said.

"Yes. It's pretty much what those women in the bar told you," Gabi said. "Alma was going around her factory floor, trying to organize the other women there. The boss warned her about it, but she kept it up. Ricardo was doing the same thing with the men. When Alma got killed, Ricardo decided that he had to disappear and blow the whistle."

"And he found April Lennox," I said.

"He didn't trust the Mexican newspapers," Gabi said. "Mrs. Esposito said he thought almost everybody in Mexico was in bed with the government and the employers."

"Some of those Mexican papers are pretty gutsy these days," I said. "He might have missed a good bet."

"He thought an American reporter would be safer," Gabi said. Her voice, excited when she called, now sounded tired. "If a Mexican reporter crossed the powers that be, they'd kill him. He told Mrs. Esposito that reporters in the States don't get murdered."

"Thanks for all this, Gabi. It's way above and beyond."

"No problem, partner. What about Dickie?"

"I'm not ready to rule him out," I said. "He's mean, and he parted badly with April. Or so Jon Cartwright said."

"I've got some other ideas for digging around here in L.A.," Gabi said. "Stay out of trouble, will you?"

"Too late," I said. "I can't help myself."

"Four Tops, 1965," she said. "Good night, sugar pie, honey bunch."

CHAPTER 27

TOMÁS PUENTE, O'MARA'S COLLEAGUE AT HOMICIDE, OFFICIALLY notified Mrs. Esposito of her nephew's death. He did it early in the day, giving him time to feed the announcement to Tucson's afternoon newspaper. The story was short, but it made the front page of the home edition. The television stations, true to form, pounced on the newspaper item. They cobbled together some file video from the riot, interviewed a police spokesman, then did live reports from Fourth Avenue or police headquarters. The story led all three evening newscasts.

"The chase is on," O'Mara said.

He was drinking a pint of Bass Ale and eating a huge plate of spicy Buffalo wings at a sports bar on Oracle Road. All the other TVs were showing sports events. O'Mara had badged the bartender and said he needed one set tuned to the news for official police business.

"I think that plate's designed for two people, O'Mara," I said.

"Damn right," he said. "I do the work of two people. Goddam city budget cuts."

"You'll probably need a second beer," I said. "I'll buy."

"There's hope for you, after all, Brinker," he said. "And you're going to solve the Juan Doe murder for us."

"Ricardo Esposito. How am I going to solve it?"

O'Mara finished his pint just as the bartender appeared with another.

"Easy," he said. "I watch you. And when some guy blows your shit away, I arrest him."

"Glad to be so helpful," I said.

"We'll arrange for a posthumous medal," he said.

"Lots of people are mad at me, O'Mara."

"Sure. I am, too, sometimes. But nobody's madder than whoever took out Mr. Esposito and Ms. Lennox. Because of you snooping around, we ID our Juan Doe and it's maybe a labor beef at the *maquilas.* The guy who comes after you will be up to his ass in this."

"I may get him before he gets me," I said.

"Right," O'Mara said. "Well, don't do it in the Tucson city limits, okay? I'd have to haul you in. It'd be a shame if the only guy to get arrested in this is you."

"Don't worry," I said. "I'm fleeing your jurisdiction tonight."

"Buen viaje," he said.

VICENTE WAS WAITING AT THE BOOKSTORE WHEN I WALKED ACROSS the border. He seemed absorbed in a paperback with a garish cover, but I knew that he was aware of everything moving nearby. I turned the corner, ducked into the first little beer joint on the right, and took a small table at the back. The barman just nodded. Five minutes later, Vicente walked in. He picked up two bottles of Corona at the bar and carried them to the table.

"Only one shift today," he said. "Ended at five o'clock. Brooks himself didn't come in. Meeting in Phoenix, apparently. The last assistant managers trickled out about six-thirty. Work starts again at eight tomorrow. The first managers come in about seven. So there's plenty of time for us to go in there."

"Security?" I said.

"Not a big issue," Vicente said. "There's two watchmen. One at the main gate for the whole complex. One at the entrance to Brooks's building. I'm having them taken care of."

"I don't want any working stiffs hurt, if we can help it," I said.

"You gotta delegate authority, Brinker. But don't worry. Guard diversion is in the best hands."

We finished the beers and started down Avenida Obregón to the Amistadt complex. On a Monday night, tourist traffic was light and most bar customers were partied out from the weekend. A Nogales city police car cruised by slowly. The young officer in the right seat gave Vicente a mock salute and a sly smile as the car moved past us.

"Friends in low places," Vicente said. "Great song."

I looked at him with surprise and he smiled. He checked his watch when we came opposite the complex entrance.

"Six minutes," he said.

We stepped into the shadowed doorway of a *farmacia,* closed for the night. From across the street, Amistadt looked like any light industrial site in North America. The several factory buildings seemed substantial enough but temporary, the kind of metal structure that could be taken down here and easily reassembled in whatever country tolerated even lower wages. You expected them to be dim, dirty, and noisy inside. But I knew from my own visit that they were cooled in summer and heated in winter, and clean, and that workers used state-of-the-art equipment as they produced goods to American and European specifications.

A chain-link fence, eight feet high with angled barbed wire at the top, stretched around the complex. From my position, I could see several sliding gates, but only one was open tonight. A small sheet metal guardhouse was on the left as visitors approached. One man stood at the doorway, leaning against the fence, looking about as alert as a night watchman can. He had no visible sidearm.

"That's it?" I said. "That's the security?"

"If it was my company, we'd have a couple of guys with Uzis there, and a big coffeepot," Vicente said. "These turkeys don't think that way."

"Let's hope they don't," I said.

We stood quietly in the doorway. Vicente put a cigarette in his mouth, but didn't light it. He checked his watch again. Down the street, two young women, staggering a bit and laughing, turned the corner and approached the Amistadt gate. Each woman carried a bottle. From the colors, I guessed that one was tequila and one was scotch or bourbon.

"You're kidding," I said.

"I needed experienced personnel with site knowledge," Vicente said.

The watchman beamed as Frida and María chatted him up.

They each offered him their liquor. He went for the tequila, took a long pull, and did not return the bottle. The women giggled and snuggled up, easing the man back into the guardhouse. Just before they got inside, I saw Frida reach for the man's belt buckle.

"Proud moment for our side," I said.

"You want nobility, join the Salvation Army," Vicente said. "You told me you want to crash the place, and you don't want anybody hurt. That poor sap is gonna drink good booze, even if it is drugged. He might even manage a little sex with two sincerely hot babes before he passes out in a few minutes, and he'll sleep like a baby. Except for being mugged, this is the best night of his life. What's wrong with that?"

We could see nothing in the guardhouse window. Frida and María and the watchman were below it. Vicente and I watched for what seemed like an hour. Eventually, Frida rose up, stepped outside, and motioned us over. We ran across the street. Frida hugged us both quickly. Her eyes shone with the thrill of it, and probably some chemical enhancement supplied by Vicente.

"*Muy fácil,*" she said. Very easy.

In the guardhouse, María stood up. I saw the unconscious watchman on the floor, his pants down around his feet.

Vicente ran to the guardhouse and turned off the light. He pushed the button that opened the electric gate. He grabbed both women's hands and pulled them inside the fence. I ran right behind them.

"The other switch is behind the guardhouse," Vicente said. "We can close the gate from this side."

I found the switch and pushed the button. The gate screeched as it began to close. Vicente, Frida, and María ran toward Building

One, where Carl Brooks kept his office. I watched the gate slam closed, then followed them.

"Ernesto is on duty at Building One tonight," Frida said. "He would give anything just to look down my dress. If I let him tonight, he'll pass out."

"If that doesn't do it, I got a sap in my pocket," Vicente said. "Let's go."

We slowed to a walk and turned the corner near the entrance to Building One. Frida took Vicente's arm and María held mine.

Ernesto was a six-footer. He looked heavy but solid. He straightened up as we approached.

"Hey, you girls are not working tonight," he said in Spanish. "And who are these guys?"

"Our friends," Frida said. "It's okay. They have permission."

"Do I look stupid?" Ernesto said, putting his bulk in the entranceway. "Nobody told me about any permission."

"Ernesto," Frida said, moving up to him. "Come here. I got something to show you."

She turned him with her right arm around his waist. Her left hand reached for the top button on her blouse. For a moment, his back was to us. Ernesto stared down at her and smiled. Then he must have remembered that if it seems too good to be true, it probably is. He was turning around when Vicente brought the sap down. Ernesto's legs buckled under him and he fell straight down. His head rested at Frida's feet.

"It's good you knocked him out," Frida said. "If he looked *up* my dress, the excitement would kill him."

We walked up a half flight of stairs to the balcony. Brooks's office door opened when I turned the knob.

"Amazing," I said. "Two doofus guards and no lock on the door."

"Overconfidence," Vicente said.

"Or they have some security gizmos we don't know about," I said.

I turned on the light. The secretary's desk occupied the first room. We could see Brooks's office through an open connecting door. Behind the secretary's desk were eight metal cabinets, each with four drawers.

"Oh, brother," I said.

"That's security, Mexico style," Vicente said. "Even thieves can never find what they want in all the paperwork."

"Let's start in the other room," I said.

"How much mess you want to make?" Vicente asked.

"Doesn't matter. When the guards come around, Brooks will know that somebody got in here."

"Thing is," Vicente said, "if this looks like a plain old robbery or vandalism, then maybe they don't tumble to what you're really looking for."

"They'll know," I said.

Brooks had a rotary Rolodex on his desktop. The *C* names were on top. I flipped through the cards. He had a number for Miguel Calderón at the U.S. Consulate. That made sense. Any American businessperson in Nogales would. I flipped to *D*.

"Bingo," I said. "Beginner's luck."

Vicente was rummaging through a file drawer behind the desk. He looked up.

"Sam Doyle," I said. "Just a phone number. But it proves that Brooks knows Doyle. We're on the right track."

"Lotta papers in here, Brinker. What's next?"

"Look for personnel files," I said. "Anything about Ricardo Esposito."

María stood in the doorway, watching us. "Look for Alma, too," she said.

"What was Alma's family name?" I asked.

"Aragón," María said. "Alma Aragón."

"Good," I said. "You and Frida look through the cabinets in there. See if they have files with names of employees on the tabs. Pull out Alma's and Ricardo's, if you find them. Then look for any of the other girls who got murdered."

"Vicente," I said, "how long are the guards going to be out?"

"The guy at the front, he'll sleep for a couple of hours, at least. The one downstairs, I may have to give him another little tap in fifteen minutes or so."

"Send Frida down there to keep an eye on him. She can run up here if he seems to be waking up."

Vicente nodded and went into the secretary's room to get Frida. I heard the door opening and Frida's high heels clicking along the balcony. María came through the connecting doorway, holding two manila file folders.

"Alma and Ricardo," she said.

Alma Aragón's personnel file looked straightforward. The first page included her employment application. The next was a photocopy of her government and employee identification cards. The third page was a work history. It showed Alma's start date and pay, a pay increase six months later. A handwritten entry from three months ago read, "Cautioned re improper employee activity." The notation was initialed "CB" and dated. The final entry was "Deceased," with the date that Alma's body was discovered and identified. The last page in the folder was a Nogales newspaper clipping about the murder.

Ricardo Esposito's file seemed similar. His work history included more notes of cautions for improper activities. The final entry, in Brooks's hand but undated, read, "Deceased."

"Are you sure he wasn't here today?" I asked Vicente.

"Had the place watched all day," he said. "Brooks never came in. I called the office here and the girl said he was in Phoenix all day."

"Today's the first day he could have known about Ricardo," I said. "The cops didn't let the news out until this morning."

"The smoking gun, almost," Vicente said.

"I'll bet Brooks wrote this on the night of the basketball riot, or maybe the next day," I said. "Somebody called and told him it was done."

I looked around the room, wondering what I had missed when I was here before. Something had bothered me then, but I never pinned it down. The group photographs with employees and company directors, the Razorbacks football pennant, the family snapshots. Nothing clicked. Perhaps it had been something about Brooks himself.

María, behind me, began to cry softly. She had Alma's file open to her friend's picture. Vicente put his arm around her, but she pulled away. She picked up the framed photograph of Brooks and his family and threw it against the wall. The frame and glass shattered and crashed to the floor.

"Let's go," I said.

Vicente steered the sobbing María out to the balcony. We hurried downstairs. Frida was watching Ernesto. He was still out cold. I pulled Vicente aside.

"These women can never come back here," I said.

"I thought of that," Vicente said. "Hector said he can get something for them."

"So they're going into the drug business."

"Hector figured you'd say that," Vicente said. "But the business didn't look so bad to you when you needed help tonight."

I said nothing. Across the hall, Frida and María were looking down at the unconscious Ernesto and giggling about something.

"They wanted to help," Vicente said. "They've seen their friends get fucked over, one way or another, for their whole lives. They know what they're doing, Brinker. Besides, Hector meant something at the restaurant for them."

"They'll have his protection?"

"Yeah."

"The Amistadt guys will know that?"

"Yeah."

We walked out of the building and across the drive to the front gate. The watchman still lay crumpled on the guardhouse floor, snoring.

"Maybe you could do something for him and Ernesto, too," I said.

"Yeah, a couple of real professionals there," Vicente said.

"At least we could pull his pants up," I said. "I hate to have these guys take a fall for us. It's tough to lose a job in this town. They'd be 'don't hire' at every place in the *maquila* association."

Vicente thought about it for a minute.

"Okay," he said. "I'll send over some guys with handcuffs and gags. Then these jerks can claim the cops did it."

Frida and María stepped into the guardhouse. With surprising strength, Frida lifted the man at the waist. María pulled his trousers up. Frida fastened his belt.

"Looks better for him this way," Frida said. She took María's arm and the four of us walked away in the cool quiet darkness of the Nogales night.

CHAPTER 28

THE NEXT MORNING, I CALLED O'MARA AND ASKED HIM TO RUN A check on Carl Brooks.

"He lives in Green Valley now," I said. "But check for Arkansas. He might have lived there before."

"Better him than me," O'Mara said. "Give me a couple of hours."

I turned on my computer and went online. On Google, I matched Brooks's name with Arkansas and Amistadt. The search came up almost empty. One listed page appeared to be an article from a Little Rock newspaper, but when I clicked on the link, an error message appeared.

Gabriela Corona went to work early, I knew. I called her office number in Los Angeles. When she answered, I said, "'Cindy's Birthday.'"

"You're kidding," Gabi said.

"No. Come on, now. It was Top Ten."

"But it's so wimpy," she said.

"You don't know it, do you? You're stalling for time to think of the name."

"Johnny Crawford," she said. "He was Chuck Connors's kid on *The Rifleman*."

"Not bad," I said.

"Not bad?" Gabi said. "It was brilliant. Now, what does winning this bet cost me?"

"You get to run a name on Nexis for me. Carl Brooks. Match it with Amistadt Enterprises or Arkansas."

Over the phone line, I heard her typing. After a moment, she said, "Got a few. Let's see. The latest one is a business brief from Little Rock. 'Plant manager to head Mexico factories.' It's just a couple of lines. 'Carl Brooks, thirty-seven, plant manager for Springville Poultry, named manager for Amistadt Enterprises operations in Nogales, Sonora, Mexico.' That your guy?"

"That's the guy."

"And you think he's doing the dirty work?"

"He practically documented it."

"Oh, boy," Gabi said. "Don't even tell me where you got the documents."

"Brooks probably didn't do the killing himself," I said. "I'm betting on that guy Doyle, the one who tailed me into Mexico. A hood who moves back and forth across the border. He actually had a file marked 'Lennox' on his desk down at East Twelfth Street. But Doyle seems to have fallen off the planet."

She said, "You're going to use Brooks to get to Doyle."

"It occurred to me," I said.

"Let me just skim back through the summaries here. The next one looks like he chaired some United Way thing in Springville. Here's a plant expansion in Springville. Chickens are big in Arkansas, I think. Oh, here's a good one. 'Union abandons Springville effort.'"

"Read that one for me, Gabi."

"I have a story meeting in a minute," she said. "Let me e-mail this to you, okay?"

"Thanks," I said. "You're a gem."

"And seriously undervalued," she said. "Hold on a sec, Brink. Other line." She clicked off, but came back in half a minute.

"Guess who's calling me?" she said.

"Why do I think it's Dickie Ungerlieder?"

"He wants to apologize."

"What did you tell him?"

"I told him to hang on," she said.

"Don't mess with that guy, Gabi," I said.

"I'm a big girl," she said. "Chicken Man is in your e-mail. So long, Brinker."

She sent a long message. The story used Springville Poultry as an example of several long-running unionization disputes at Arkansas poultry plants. A food workers' union tried to organize Springville Poultry, but employees voted to remain nonunion. Union leaders accused Brooks of unfair labor practices, including unlawful obstruction of union recruiting and intimidation of workers. The complaints were dismissed.

The article quoted Brooks as saying, "We simply did not believe that creating a union environment was in the best interests of our company, our fine employees, and our community. We were pleased to see that view vindicated in the vote." A labor analyst at the University of Arkansas predicted that employers would give Brooks credit for holding down costs by retaining Springville's nonunion status. The analyst said, "He's known as a hardball player who meets corporate goals."

Just the guy to keep uppity workers in Mexico under control, I thought. Sure enough, two months after his victory at Springville, Brooks took the Amistadt job. It's a long way from union-busting to murder, though. The new information fit what I knew about Brooks, but did not move me closer to proving what I suspected.

O'Mara called back at ten o'clock. "No arrests, no nothing," he said. "The guy could get a security clearance, far as I can tell."

Brooks's business card was on the table. I called the Nogales office number. A woman answered, "*Buenos días.* Mr. Brooks's office." I heard bustling sounds and men's voices behind her.

"This is Brinker," I said. "Mr. Brooks, please."

"Just a moment, please, sir," she said. The phone went on hold. There was a click, and I knew that someone was on the line in a quieter room.

"Brinker," Brooks said. There was no smile in his voice this time. "I was just thinking about you."

"Why is that?" I asked.

"Somebody trashed my office last night and took files involving employees of ours who died recently. You were asking about such people when you visited me."

"I'd like to talk more about that," I said.

"Why don't you come down here?" he said. "You know the way to the office."

"I don't think so," I said. "Let's meet on the U.S. side, in some nice public place."

He didn't answer. I listened for a whisper to someone else with him in the room, but I heard nothing.

"What do you say, Brooks?"

"All right," he said. "There's a steak house off I-19, just south of Green Valley. You know the place?"

"Yes."

"The bar is pretty quiet in the late afternoon. I'll be there about six."

"Okay," I said.

"Just you, right?" he said.

"Just me. You can bring Doyle, if you want."

"I don't know any Doyle," he said. "Six o'clock."

CHAPTER 29

A DILAPIDATED COVERED WAGON SAT IN FRONT OF THE STEAK HOUSE. The building affected an old western ranch style, with weathered plank siding and hitching posts at the entrance. It was close to town, on the corner of a big shopping center property, and frequented by locals. If Brooks had homicidal thoughts, I didn't think he would act them out in front of his neighbors.

He came in promptly at six and spotted me sitting at a small booth in the far corner of the bar. About ten other customers were in the room, but none within three tables of mine. The waitress appeared as he slid into the booth opposite me.

"Glenlivet, rocks," he said. I already had a Dos Equis.

Neither of us spoke again until the waitress returned with his drink, gave us a little bowl of pretzels, and left. Brooks drank half of his whiskey, put down the glass, and looked at me.

"How do I know you're not recording this?" he said.

"Wearing a wire, as seen on TV?" I said.

"Whatever."

"Well, I'm not. But it doesn't matter. We're having this conversation anyway."

"If you ever set foot in Mexico again," he said, "I'll have you arrested. I don't know about extradition from Arizona for burglary and theft of company property, but I'm looking into that."

"Interesting," I said. "Filed a complaint with the police, have you?"

He drained his glass and signaled the waitress for another.

I said, "Did your complaint explain what was missing, and why a thief might have wanted it?"

Even in the gloom of the bar, I could see his face redden. It might have been caused by chugging single-malt scotch or by anger.

"I wonder," I said, "if the missing property involved murder victims who were members of your happy little *maquila* family."

His second drink arrived. He sipped at this one, then seemed to drop the tough-guy pose. He looked at me like one reasonable man making a deal with another.

"I have a real family, you know," he said. "My wife and I have been married for fifteen years. We were college sweethearts and got married right after we graduated. My boy is eleven and my little girl is nine."

"Ricardo Esposito and Alma Aragón were sweethearts, too," I said. "They probably would have married and had kids."

"You don't think I killed them?" Brooks said.

"Maybe," I said. "Either way, you know who did, and how, and why. And your only prayer to salvage anything from this is to tell me everything."

A couple in tennis togs waved as they walked to a table across the room. Brooks managed an empty smile and waved back.

"What makes you think I know anything about them?" he asked.

"For one thing," I said, "you knew that Esposito was dead before anyone else did. And you understand how I know that, don't you?"

He finished the second scotch and leaned back against the wall of the booth. His shoulders slumped and his face looked as though he hadn't slept for days. I thought he might cry.

"I have to think," he said. "Please don't do anything until I sort this out. Will you promise me that?"

"No," I said.

Brooks nodded, pushed himself up from the booth, and walked out without another word.

I DROVE HOME IN THE TWILIGHT. COMMUTERS RACED SOUTH FROM Tucson, an unbroken stream of oncoming cars, all going seventy. My mood darkened with the evening as I thought of April Lennox, gone, and Carl Brooks, still here and worrying about his family. I wondered if some Amistadt stakeholder was whispering into a transatlantic telephone, "Will no one rid me of this meddlesome private detective?" I wondered if Sam Doyle had fallen in behind me on the freeway, ready to do his unknown master's tacit bidding. But no lights appeared behind me as I circled my neighborhood twice and finally pulled into my garage.

Al had brought me a big pot of Anna's *albóndigas* soup. I put some on the stove to warm. I imagined Anna, happy to feed her extended family, chopping the carrots and celery, rolling the ground pork and beef into little balls. The aroma filled the room and I could see her there, looking over her shoulder and smiling at Al and the girls and me.

I ate the soup and a roll. I pulled on a Wildcat basketball sweatshirt, a souvenir of the championship season. That sight of that shirt always brought back the cheers from Arizona's victory. Now it made me think of another Final Four game night when Ricardo Esposito died.

The sky was clear and filled with stars. I pushed open the door to the back yard and walked out there with a bottle of wine. It was the McManis cabernet again. One glass tonight. April Lennox, who first brought the wine, was gone. Dolores had chosen to be a continent away. Gabi Corona, who might have chosen to be here, loved L.A. None of them was with me, and I wondered if one ever would.

I HAD FINISHED THE BOTTLE AND FALLEN ASLEEP OUTSIDE. MORNING coffee didn't help. Neither did aspirin. My head was still thick at ten o'clock when O'Mara called my cell phone.

"Damnedest thing," he said. "I went out to the sheriff's this morning. Interagency breakfast, you know, to compare cases. See if any of us is barking up the same tree and don't know it."

"Don't tell me," I said. "You found the real killers for O.J."

"Nope," he said. "County picks up a homicide last night. Parking lot of the shopping center just south of Green Valley. Looks like the guy was popped right in his car, out there in the corner of the lot. Detectives ask around. You know that old western steak joint? Seems the waitress can ID the vic as two quick Glevlivets on the rocks. And his friend who paid the tab was a big guy. Sounds a lot like someone I know. But what really perked me up was the vic's name."

"Yeah," I said. "Carl Brooks."

"The same Carl Brooks I ran for you yesterday?"

"The very same."

"Lots of people getting dead in your vicinity," O'Mara said.

"I think I did something stupid," I said. "I scared him, and somebody decided that he was too much of a risk."

"Whatever you did," O'Mara said, "we have to get together pronto. You and me and my friend from the sheriff's. Where are you right now?"

"Back at square one," I said.

CHAPTER 30

THE COUNTY HOMICIDE DETECTIVE, GUILLERMO SMITH, MET US AT O'Mara's office downtown. O'Mara called him Bill. Smith wore crisp, clean blue jeans and a white golf shirt that showed off his time in the gym. Either his hair was prematurely gray or his face was improbably young. His expression never changed. He asked no questions as I gave him my edited story. But he had the hard eyes of a cop who had been lied to plenty and was sick of it.

When I finished recounting my meeting with Carl Brooks, Smith said, "So you felt pretty strongly about the April Lennox murder." His soft voice had no accent of Mexico.

"Yes," I said.

"You'd been investigating it for a while?"

"Yes. When O'Mara told me that nobody on either side of the border was paying much attention to it."

"And what made you set up the appointment with Brooks for yesterday?"

I tried to answer quickly. Mentioning our break-in at Amistadt seemed like a bad idea.

"So much points to that *maquila* company," I said. "There are other leads, but it seemed like the strongest. Several of the Nogales victims worked there. April died the same way those women did. Two employees told me that Brooks cracked the whip on Ricardo Esposito and Alma Aragón for their organizing activity. He was the only real connection between April's death and the others."

Smith watched me closely as I spoke. I don't think those hard cop eyes even blinked.

"You visited Brooks at his office last week, right?" Smith said.

"Right. Friday afternoon."

"And you heard from the two employees when?"

"Friday night."

"So what in particular happened between Friday and last night that made you put the pressure on Brooks?"

"Nothing," I said. "It was a busy weekend. I went to Los Angeles to interview a guy who knew April."

"Convenient," he said.

"Come on, Smith," I said. "Yes, I cared about April Lennox, and yes, I think Brooks was involved in her death somehow. But I don't blow people away on suspicion. And I sure don't do it a few minutes after meeting the guy in a public place and buying him drinks."

"Maybe not," Smith said.

O'Mara shrugged and said, "He's not a complete and total moron, Bill."

"Another good reference," Smith said. "So Brinker, what do you, in your innocence, think happened?"

"Only one thing makes sense to me," I said. "Somebody with a big stake in this mess followed him to the restaurant. They waited for him to come out. They got in his car with him, talked to him, figured he was scared shitless, and killed him. They left him there, walked over to their own car, and left."

Smith stood up and looked down at me. "Not bad," he said. "It's my second-choice scenario, in fact. Stay handy, Brinker."

He nodded to O'Mara and left the room. O'Mara rolled his shoulders. I could hear something pop.

"Guillermo Smith," he said. "What the hell kind of name is that?"

"Anglo dad, Hispanic mom," I said.

"Ridiculous," he said. "Can you see me naming a kid Guillermo O'Mara?"

"You? No."

"Anyway, I've only been out here for fifteen years," he said. "I don't think Señor Smith trusts me yet."

"Whoever clipped Brooks got a twofer," I said. "He took out a potential liability, and put some heat on me."

"Picked a good place, too," O'Mara said. "You're not connected with the sheriffs like you are with us because of Captain Avila. Smith probably doesn't think you did it, but he's not ready to rule you out."

"It's got to be Doyle," I said. "He does the dirty work. The tails, the threats. They all come through him."

"If Brooks is gone," O'Mara said, "who does Doyle work for now?"

"Doyle might not know," I said. "Let's see who shows up to run the Amistadt *maquilas*."

I CALLED VICENTE FROM MY CAR. WHEN HE ANSWERED, I HEARD water running and laughter in the background.

"Giving the girls a bath," he said. "Fringe benefit of working for Hector."

"For them or for you?" I asked.

"I've got something interesting for you," he said. "I checked with a friend of mine on the local *policía*. I asked him if they had any interesting crime on the last couple of nights."

"And?"

"And they had pretty quiet tours of duty. Not too many drunk tourists early in the week. Couple of knife fights up in the *colonias*. The usual shit. But you know what? No report of a break-in at a certain business."

I heard María shout, *"¡Soy inocente!"*

"I doubt that," I said. Vicente told her and both women laughed.

"Amistadt's hushing it up," I said.

"Your pal Brooks must have made that decision," Vicente said. "Lot of good it did him."

"You hear who the new boss will be?"

"Not yet. Today they have a shop foreman from Building One in charge. A local guy. But the word is that some Amistadt big shot will be in tomorrow or the next day."

"Can you keep an eye on the place?"

"Already being done, Brinker."

"Hector's okay with this?" I asked. "I feel as though you're working full-time for me."

"It's Hector's town," Vicente said. "He likes to know what's happening in the other major industries here. You're an investment."

CHAPTER 31

WE FELT SUMMER COMING. IN SPRING, CRISP AIR LINGERED WELL after the sun rose. Now, coolness dissolved at first light. Every creature in the desert knew that we'd be cooking soon.

When Gabi Corona called me late in the afternoon, I was sitting at my kitchen table, writing down my questions and answers about April's murder. The question column stretched to a second page. The answer list was short. What happened to Doyle lately? Was Dickie Ungerlieder or Jon Cartwright the liar, or both of them? What did any of these guys have to do with Ricardo Esposito's murder or April Lennox's?

"Come see me," Gabi said. She usually spoke with that salsa smile in her voice. Not today. She seemed to have trouble sounding out the words. No gags about old songs, either.

"I can't get over to L.A. again, Gabi," I said.

"You don't have to," she said.

THE CORONA HOUSE WAS WEST OF I-10, JUST NORTH OF DOWN-town Tucson. People called it a poor neighborhood, but they weren't looking closely. The homes and yards, however small and inexpensively built, were well kept. No old cars languished in the driveways. No gangs of kids roamed the sidewalks, hoping for trouble. Gabi's parents had bought the house three years before she was born. Her car, the little sedan with California plates, was parked on the street out front.

Jesús Corona met me at the door. He was short and solid, with the quiet warmth of so many Mexican workingmen. He would be sixty or so by now. His hair had turned pure white, but his face somehow remained unlined despite years of carpentry in the Tucson sun.

"We don't see you much anymore," he said. "We read about you when you got shot at the border, but that's been a while."

"I'm glad to have that way behind me," I said.

As I started into the house, he held my arm and drew me back to the porch.

"You know," he said, "Gabi was the first one in our family to go to college. Her mother and I were so proud when she graduated from high school. That was a first, too. Then the U of A, and a scholarship. We were thrilled. And she had a good job here, and then the wonderful offer in Los Angeles."

"She's good," I said. "She earned it all. You have every right to be proud."

"Yes," he said. "But we worry. It's a crazy place over there. Los

Diablos might be a better name. More devils than angels." He allowed himself a little smile, making sure that I got his joke.

I nodded and waited for him to continue.

"Whatever she did over there," Jesús Corona said, "I won't meddle. She's a woman and it's no longer my place to make her choices. But a father always cares. Don't encourage her to put herself in danger, Brink. Let her live the life that she earned. Please let her mother and me take pleasure in that."

It was so simple and loving and logical that I had no answer for him. He knew. He patted my back and gave me a push toward the door. "Go see her," he said.

I walked into the front room. Gabi sat in her father's big chair, the one facing the television and the window. Her lower lip was split, the dark scab forming in the center of an angry red wound. Her right eye was black. Her right cheekbone looked as if someone had run coarse sandpaper over it. Her left wrist was in a cast.

Behind me, Jesús Corona said, "I'm going to get your mother at the dentist, Gabi. We'll be back in an hour or so."

"Okay, Papa," she said. She held up her left wrist and said to me, "I'll have to type with my toes for a while."

I went to her and pulled an ottoman over to the chair, facing her.

"Was this Dickie?" I said.

"I don't know. I came home from work the other night. My apartment building has little carports for us in the back. It was dark. There was nobody around, but it's a pretty safe neighborhood. I got out of my car, and just as I shut the door, somebody grabbed me from behind. It was a big guy. Too big to be Dickie."

"Too much coincidence for anything else, though."

"Yeah," she said. "At first, I thought it was your basic L.A. mugging. But this guy wasn't grabbing anything. I had my purse on my shoulder and car keys in my hand. He just punched me in the eye and the mouth, then he held my arm and said, 'Quit snooping, bitch.' He snapped my wrist like a pencil and pushed me down on the ground. That's when I got the scrapes, I think. By the time I looked up, he was gone."

"You see his face?"

"No. There's almost no light out there. He had a Dodgers cap pulled down pretty low. And it happened so quickly. I couldn't tell you anything about him, except he was a big, heavy guy who could move fast. He had a really revolting aftershave. He had short hair, like a crew cut. It rubbed my neck when he was bending over, holding me. And he had a big ruby ring on his left ring finger. He put his hand around my neck. The hand was so big that I could see the ring."

Gabi sat back in her father's chair. She seemed worn out from talking about it.

"Gotta be working for Dickie," I said.

"Maybe," she said. "Probably. I couldn't prove it."

"You call the cops?" I said.

"Sure. They were nice. But you know, a little mugging, just one broken bone. That's like crossing on the DON'T WALK sign to cops there. Anyway, they got me to the emergency room. Then I called Papa. He flew over and drove me home. Home, here."

I reached out and took her undamaged hand.

"There, there," she said. "It'll be okay."

"You could have called me," I said.

"Sometimes Papa's just the right thing, you know? And Mama had the *sopa de lima con pollo* ready when we came in the front door."

"Okay," I said. "No argument there."

"You know," she said, "riding home, I saw a sign on the freeway, right at the Colorado River. It says, YOU ARE NOW LEAVING CALIFORNIA. RESUME NORMAL BEHAVIOR."

I laughed despite my anger at Dickie and guilt about Gabi.

"Don't be so damn composed," I said. "You do a favor for me and you get your bones cracked."

"I have a friend at the paper with carpal tunnel syndrome that hurts worse than this," she said, raising her cast a little. "And she doesn't even have any colorful stories about it."

She tried to smile, but managed only a little one. I could see that the effort hurt, what with the split lip and the bruised cheek.

"I'm going to do something about this," I said.

"My hero," Gabi said. "Don't play Señor Macho, Brinker. If this was Dickie, he hired professional muscle to beat up a woman. God knows what he'll have waiting for you. And if you get on him over there, I imagine the Malibu sheriffs favor the local beachfront landowners."

"One way or another," I said, "somebody pays for this."

"What if it wasn't Dickie?" she said. "How about that guy who was following you around?"

"Sam Doyle."

"Yes. Maybe he's still watching you and knew that I was working with you."

"I don't see how he could have, Gabi. I didn't advertise my trip to L.A. to see Dickie. Even if Doyle had been tailing me, he couldn't have come on the same plane. I would have seen him."

"He could have called somebody in L.A. to pick up your trail when you got there."

"Sounds like a stretch," I said. "Sometimes the obvious answer is right. My money's on Dickie."

Gabi took a prescription medicine bottle from the table beside her. She shook out two pills and swallowed them with orange juice.

"I tried to think of all the old 'hurt' songs I could use on you," she said. "But I take these and it doesn't hurt so bad."

"'Hurt So Bad,'" I said. "Little Anthony and the Imperials."

"I don't know if the Imperials were on that one," she said. "They might have broken up."

"It happens," I said.

CHAPTER 32

VICENTE KNEW THE COUPLE WHO RAN THE STORE ACROSS THE street from the Amistadt factories. The little grocery had a small storeroom at the side. We stood at the tiny window, looking through the burglar bars to the street. I noticed that the new Amistadt guard looked like a serious soldier, in shape and armed with a handgun in a gleaming black holster.

"The word is," Vicente said, "the new guy comes in at nine A.M. They have a little welcoming committee of workers over by the entrance to Building One."

"We might not be able to see him from here," I said.

"*No importa,* dude," Vicente said. "Frida and María have a couple of cutie pie friends who got picked for the welcome wagon. One of them just happens to have a digital camera. We'll get a report with pictures as soon as things break up."

"You're a man of many talents."

"Not me. Frida and María thought of it. I think Hector's gonna make them executive vice presidents, the rate they're going."

"The land of opportunity," I said.

Two Nogales cops on motorcycles passed our window and turned into the Amistadt gate. The new guard waved them straight in. A police van was next, carrying six officers. A black Cadillac sedan with an Arizona license plate came right behind. We could not see through its tinted windows. The guard saluted as the car glided by. Two more cops on cycles followed.

"Courtesy escort would just be two bikes," Vicente said. "That motorcade is security. Watch. The cops in the van will be in position, spread around, before anyone gets out of the Caddy."

He was right. As the caravan approached Building One, the first motorcycles split up and turned 180 degrees to face out toward the gate. The van cut to one side and stopped next to the welcoming committee. All six officers hurried out and took up positions, blocking part of our view. They looked ceremonial, standing at parade rest in their crisp uniforms, but each man was in top shape and all had sidearms.

The trailing motorcycle cops stopped behind the Cadillac. They leapt off their bikes and trotted to the car's rear doors. A man stepped out from the right front. He was six-five, I figured, and weighed 270, and sported a buzz cut. His crisply creased gray slacks were a little too tight. His cream-colored guayabera shirt was worn outside. With a guy like him, that usually meant a gun on the hip beneath the shirt. His left hand was in his pants pocket.

All the cops watched a distinguished Mexican man in a black suit who stood at the front of the welcoming group.

"El alcalde," Vicente said. The mayor.

On the mayor's signal, the policemen opened the car's rear doors in unison. Two men climbed out, one from each side. They straightened their suit coats and walked straight to the mayor. Everyone shook hands. The welcoming committee applauded. Several cameras flashed in rapid succession. From our distance and angle, we could see only the visitors' backs.

"Never fear," Vicente said. "We'll have the front view in a few minutes."

The welcome ceremony went quickly. After a moment of chat, two little girls in identical frilly pink dresses brought bouquets of flowers to the new arrivals. Both men bent down to give the girls grandfatherly hugs, then the children scurried back to the other greeters. The mayor pointed the way to Building One. The VIPs and three other men walked in that direction. All the police gathered at the van and began talking and laughing.

A young woman with a camera in her hand walked casually to the gate, giving her butt a little wiggle for the guard when she passed him. She crossed the street and entered the grocery store.

"Jugo de naranja, por favor," we heard her say.

"Sí señorita," the grocer answered. We heard the old cash register clang. A moment later, we could see the woman returning to the Amistadt gate, carrying only a small plastic container of orange juice. She looked over her shoulder and winked.

The grocer carried the camera into our storeroom.

"A su servicio, Vicente," he said. At your service.

"Mi jefe le da las gracias, amigo," Vicente said. Hector thanks you, my friend. The grocer beamed.

AT THE APARTMENT, VICENTE'S COMPUTER SCREEN GLOWED. He connected the camera to the computer with a short cable and fiddled with the photo settings. Up came a vibrant image of the two men from the Cadillac striding forward to greet the mayor. Both were handsome in their dark suits, white shirts, and ties. The younger man had copper-brown skin and thick black hair. I made him for a Mexican manager, probably the replacement for Brooks. The older man had a good tan but was not Hispanic. His hair was thinning and blond. An executive of Amistadt, perhaps from Germany.

"You know them?" Vicente asked.

"The older guy on the left is familiar, but I don't know where I've seen him. The young guy, I have no clue."

Vicente hit a key and the next picture appeared. This one was closer to the men. I still couldn't place them. The third photo showed the two men and the mayor, all facing the camera, with the building behind them.

"Last one," Vicente said, and we saw the men bending down to thank the little flower girls. Vicente clicked back to the picture where all three men looked straight into the camera lens, flashing their broadest photo-op smiles.

"There's something about this one," I said.

"Looks like every other ribbon-cutting picture," Vicente said.

I flopped down on the couch to think about it. Too many

ideas rattling around in my brain. Too much death already, and nothing that quite tied together with anything else.

"Ribbon-cutting picture," I said.

Vicente grunted.

"That's where I saw that guy's face. The older one. I think he's in a picture that Carl Brooks had on his wall in the *maquila* office. He's some kind of director of Amistadt."

"Figures," Vicente said. "He's showing the corporate flag today."

"I need to get his name," I said.

"It'll be in the *International* tomorrow."

"I'm not waiting for the newspaper," I said. I tested my cell phone for a signal from the Arizona side. It looked good. I called the Corona home number.

A woman's soft voice answered, *"Bueno."* Josephina Corona spoke perfect English, but the old habits hang on. I told her who was calling and asked for Gabi. "Just a moment, please," she said in a tone of required politeness. I couldn't blame her.

"What's up, shamus?" Gabi said.

"You sound better," I said.

"I am. Home cooking and painkillers. Nothing like it. I'd say it's better than sex, but I don't have any recent basis for comparison."

"I hope your mother left the room."

"She's back in the kitchen."

"Do you have a computer in the house?"

"I brought my laptop," she said.

"Can you dial into the paper's news services?"

"Sure."

"Could you find coverage of an event in Nogales with Amistadt and the *maquilas*? I don't know how long ago, but it would have the board of directors in town for a grand opening or ribbon-cutting."

"Maybe," she said. "You have quite a few key words to work with. If it's out there, we probably have it."

"E-mail me a picture if there's one with the story," I said.

"Sure."

"Do you mind, Gabi? Are you up to it?"

"Oh, yeah. If I have to watch another *telenovela* with Mama, I'm going to double the painkiller dosage. This will give me an excuse to break away."

"How am I ever going to pay you back?" I asked.

"Wait till my lip heals," she said.

CHAPTER 33

VICENTE PROMISED TO CALL ME WHEN HE HEARD MORE ABOUT THE new *maquila* manager and what happened inside the plant. I walked across the border, claimed my car from the parking lot, and headed up the I-19.

So I was remembering an executive from an Amistadt photograph. So what? They owned the company. Why wouldn't a top guy be there for a ribbon-cutting or change of command? The more I learned, the less I knew.

Ten miles south of downtown Tucson, the familiar white bell towers of Mission San Xavier del Bac came into view. On a whim, I cut off the interstate and took the old road across the edge of the reservation. I don't spend much time in churches, but the dim interior of a two-hundred-year-old sanctuary seemed just the right tonic today.

I entered the tiny church and sat on one of the hard wooden

pews in the middle of the narrow room. There was much to admire in this small space, and much I could not see. Spanish angels cling to arches and Franciscan saints ride fiery chariots above the choir. But the interior light casts shadows. Only those who walk around the turns and wait for the changing light can see most of the artistry inside. Fine examples of art and devotion evade the sight of infrequent visitors like me.

European experts spent years bringing the glorious paintings and altars back to life after almost two centuries of inattention. Then they taught devoted Tohono O'odham to take charge. Somewhere on the grounds at that moment, surely an Indian was working to preserve the church they call the White Dove of the Desert.

But in the sanctuary, on a weekday afternoon out of tourist season, I was alone. No priest offered guidance. No prayers came to mind. I could not recall the name of the patron saint of the sick. I reached into my pocket and found only a twenty-dollar bill. I dropped it in the box on my way out, and whispered to myself, "For Gabi."

CHAPTER 34

"HELMUT KELLY IS THE GERMAN GUY," VICENTE SAID ON THE phone. "North American vice president for Amistadt, effectively the number one guy on this side of the Atlantic. The new manager is Gustavo Larriva. Apparently they brought him in from their Ciudad Juárez operation. How'd a German guy get to be named Kelly?"

"Maybe some Irish GI stayed in Germany after the war. Married a German girl, and along came Helmut."

"Whatever. Anyway, Helmut went around to all the buildings and gave the troops a pep talk. It was like, 'Don't listen to all the rumors. You've got a great deal here, so be happy in your work.' Apparently the *obreros* thought it meant, 'No grumbling or we can you.'"

"Is he still around?"

"No," Vicente said. "He made the goodwill tour, then spent

about an hour locked up with Larriva in the manager's office. After that, he and his bodyguard took the limo back across the border to Tucson. Apparently he's staying at the La Paloma tonight."

"Did you know the bodyguard?" I asked.

"Never seen him before," Vicente said. "He's not from around here. Doesn't work for Hector or any competitors. Probably just a Rent-a-Bruiser from one of the security agencies in Phoenix."

"I wonder," I said. "I'm down to long shots, and I just thought of one."

TWO HOURS LATER, GABRIELA CORONA AND I WERE SITTING IN A Mercedes-Benz S600, borrowed for the night from David Katz. I tossed David's *Arizona Attorney* magazines and Cessna pilot's cap into the back seat and headed for the Westin La Paloma Hotel. I parked at the left rear of the auto-entrance plaza. Anyone driving in would slip past us and pull to the right to drop off passengers or leave the car with a valet. Hotels do not mind if a gleaming top-of-the-line Mercedes is parked out front. I gave the two valets twenty bucks each and said we'd just like to sit a spell. They said, "Enjoy your evening, folks."

I had brought corned beef sandwiches and potato salad and two huge pickles and Dr. Brown's creme soda from Feig's Deli. I put on Diana Krall's *Look of Love* CD. David's car stereo sounded better than the Tucson Convention Center Music Hall.

"Thank you," Gabi said. "I'm so sick of Mexican food. God bless Mama, but one more bowl of *sopa de lima* and I'll start clucking."

"No guarantee this will work," I said. "Herr Kelly may be in for the night."

"I can wait," she said. "Sitting still is what I do best this week. What if I have to pee?"

"This car probably has a bathroom. We'll find it if we just press the right button."

We ate our sandwiches. We passed the potato salad container back and forth. We watched two couples get out of a Lexus and walk into the lobby.

"The paper's data service is down," Gabi said. "It should be up tomorrow. I'll try again in the morning."

"Time enough," I said.

"So who you think I'm going to recognize? This Kelly?"

"I don't want to tell you," I said. "If I prompt you, it might not be a solid identification. Let's just watch the nobility come and go for a while. See what happens."

Diana Krall went into the title track, with that mellow late-night saloon piano and a voice as smooth as sherry.

Gabi said, "That's nice for sitting here in the evening. But Dusty Springfield's version was better."

"True," I said. "Diana has superb legs, though."

Gabi looked at the picture on the CD case. "Some girls have all the luck," she said.

"You're being taken to dinner by a guy in a Mercedes," I said.

I could see her thinking of a comeback when the big man walked out of the lobby. He stood there for a moment, looking around. Casual, hands in pockets. His gaze passed over our car, but we were parked in shadow. I was fairly sure that he would not see us inside.

The man turned and nodded to someone in the lobby. Helmut Kelly came out. The two men turned to their right, away from us, and walked down toward the Janos restaurant at the end of the drive.

"Jesus Christ," Gabi said.

"You think it's him?"

"Maybe. More than maybe. The size and the short hair are right. I've got a really creepy feeling about that guy. I can almost smell that ugly aftershave again."

Kelly and the bodyguard were almost halfway down the drive. Above and to their left, across the parking lot, an enormous new house was under construction. The bodyguard pointed it out to Kelly, using his big left hand.

"My God," Gabi said. "Look at the ring."

"How about that?" I said. "We did something right."

I drove her home and helped her to the door. We stood on her parents' front porch, watching the freeway lights several blocks away, and listening to the soft hum of the speeding cars.

"That guy has no idea I'm here, right?" she said.

"I don't think he could," I said. "His job was to scare you off. He probably doesn't even know you're from Tucson."

"I'll take my own chances, but I don't want any of this coming down on Mama and Papa."

"It should be okay, Gabi. I'll ask Al to have a patrol car swing by here a few times tonight."

She stood on tiptoes, winced, and hugged me gingerly.

"You're a lot of fun, Brinker, if we live," she said.

CHAPTER 35

DAVID KATZ LET ME KEEP THE CAR FOR THE WEEKEND. THE NEXT morning, I tipped a new shift of valet parking attendants and took my place near the hotel entrance. At nine-thirty, Helmut Kelly and his henchman came outside together. A valet pulled the Caddy to the curb as the men arrived. A bellman scurried out with one big suitcase and put it in the trunk. Today, Bruiser drove and Kelly sat up front with him.

I hated to get behind them so quickly, but there was a traffic light at the Sunrise Drive entrance to the hotel grounds. If I failed to stay with them, I would not see which way they turned. So, hoping that a $125,000 Mercedes would be inconspicuous to such people, I fell in and followed. We turned left at the light.

They took another left at Campbell. Going to the airport, probably. Halfway down the hill to River Road, I pulled into a side street, let two cars pass me, then moved back into the traffic.

I stayed with them easily all the way to the airport. Instead of going to the main passenger dropoff ramp, Bruiser turned into the executive terminal area. He parked and grabbed the suitcase. Both men walked into the terminal.

Would either of these guys recognize me? I didn't think so. But what would be my excuse for walking in after them? I remembered David's pilot cap in the back seat. It sported a Cessna logo and an embroidered *N* number, the registration number for David's own Cessna. That would give me bona fides at any airport business. I pulled it on and headed for the door.

When I got inside, Helmut Kelly already was walking through an exit door to the tarmac. He made for a Learjet about fifty yards away. A ramp worker followed with his suitcase. Bruiser watched from a wide window.

"Help you, sir?" a young man behind the counter asked.

"Yes," I said. I leaned on the counter and turned away from Bruiser, just in case. "My wife and I are moving to Tucson next month, and I'm looking for a place to keep my 172." I was pretty sure that David had called his Cessna a 172.

"We can take it for the summer," the man said. "Winter's tighter here, of course, but I think we'll still have a spot or two this year."

I asked about hangar space and rental fees. I tried to throw in a few words David had used when he talked about his plane. The man did not look puzzled, so I must have been a fairly credible weekend pilot. Out of the corner of my eye, I could see that Bruiser was still at the window. I heard the Learjet engines cranking up.

"Well, that's great," I said. "I'll give you a call when we get to town."

He handed me a brochure and a business card. I looked out the big window, past Bruiser, and noted the *N* number on the Learjet. Then I went back to the Mercedes and waited to see where Helmut Kelly's bodyguard would lead me.

THE CADDY ROLLED WEST ON VALENCIA TOWARD I-19. I THOUGHT that Bruiser might be returning to Mexico, but he headed north on the freeway and picked up I-10 at downtown, going toward Phoenix. In just a few minutes, though, he turned at Miracle Mile, swung into the right lane, and cruised slowly past the hourly motels.

The prostitutes were out early this morning. Bruiser eased over to the curb. A plump brunette with dangerously high heels, an almost nonexistent skirt, and grotesque makeup bent down to the passenger window. They spoke for a moment, making the deal made a hundred times a day on this street. The woman got into the car. Bruiser drove forward to the next motel and pulled up to the office. The woman went in and returned a moment later with a key. She got back into the Caddy and they drove to a room at the far end of the building.

I love my job. This guy spends the night at one of the best resorts in the country, drives a captain of industry to his private jet, then picks up a street whore for a morning quickie. I pulled up to the office and went inside.

A sleepy, skinny clerk with messed-up hair and a day's beard looked at me through the bulletproof glass.

"I need the other key to that hooker's room," I said.

"Which hooker?" the clerk said.

"The one who just came in."

"You fuckin' nuts?" he said.

I pushed a hundred-dollar bill through the slot in the glass.

"That's the good news," I said. "The bad news is, if you give me any shit, Bobby Vaughan from vice will have cops doing foot patrols on your driveway for the next year."

He didn't even think about it. He grabbed a key, pushed it through the slot, and said, "Try not to make a mess, okay?"

I PUT THE KEY IN MY LEFT HAND AND MY GUN IN THE RIGHT. THE lock was a cheapie in the door handle, so I could simply insert the key, turn it, and push in. I shoved in the key, twisted it, and moved into the room in a shooting crouch.

Bruiser was standing by the bed, his trousers dropped down around his ankles. His jacket lay on the bed. I couldn't see a weapon. The hooker apparently had experienced worse or weirder things than this. She did not scream. She just stood up and looked at me. She was still fully dressed, if you could call it that.

"Out," I said to her. "Go back to work. If you say a word about this, vice will hassle you every day for the rest of your life. Did he pay you already?"

Bruiser said, "Yeah, I did." The whore looked disappointed.

"Out," I said. She grabbed her purse from the bedside table and tottered through the door.

"If you're gonna kill me," Bruiser said, "you shoulda killed her." He spoke without affect and had no accent that I recognized.

"That depends on how we do here," I said. "I know where to find her if it comes to that. Go sit in the corner there. Leave your pants down."

"I don't do guys," he said.

"I know what you do," I said. "Over there. Now."

He stumbled over to the far right corner of the small room and sat on the floor. I picked up his jacket from the bed. He kept a black leather wallet in the inside pocket. I opened it and saw the driver's license. Antonio Cazzo, Phoenix address. I put the license in my shirt pocket. I went through the rest of the jacket, but found only a cell phone. There was no weapon in sight. I looked at him.

"In the car," he said. "I put it in the trunk when we came in here."

Maybe, I thought.

"What you do, Tony," I said, "is beat up women. I want to know why you jumped a woman at an apartment building in L.A. three nights ago."

"I don't know any women in L.A."

"You didn't *know* her, but you smashed her face and broke her wrist, anyway. I don't get mad too often, Tony, but seeing a woman treated like that will do it."

He swallowed hard but matched my stare. I could see the wheels turning in his thick gangster head: Who's going to blink first here?

"It was just a job, man," he said. "If she's a friend of yours, tell her I'm sorry. Nothing personal about it."

"Unbelievable, Tony. She thought it was pretty personal. Did Helmut Kelly put you up to it?"

For the first time, something like fear flickered in his eyes.

"Come on, man," he said. "If I told you anything about Kelly and it got back to him, he'd kill me."

"Talk to me, Tony," I said, "or I'll save him the trouble."

Some of the starch went out of him. He took a big breath, exhaled with a resigned sigh, and said, "Okay, look. When Kelly comes to Arizona, California sometimes, I drive him around and watch his back. We're over in Beverly Hills the other night. He has dinner with this weaselly little investment promoter that he does some business with."

"Weaselly little guy? What's his name?"

"Dickie. Dickie Underwear or Underwater or something. I dunno. Just Dickie is what Kelly calls him."

"Dickie Ungerlieder," I said.

"Yeah, I guess that's it."

"Keep talking."

"Dickie says he has this problem. A couple of reporters come snooping around. At least, they said they were reporters. So Dickie checks and finds out the woman really is. He says they could make big problems for everybody."

"What did he mean, everybody?" I said.

"I dunno. I think he meant for Kelly and him. Kelly's company has some big trouble at a plant in Mexico. That's why he was there and in Arizona yesterday."

"And Dickie knows something about that?"

"I guess. Anyway, Dickie says to Kelly, I wish I could just make that reporter bitch and her friend disappear. Kelly says, Don't be stupid. You can't do that to reporters in this country. Dickie goes, We gotta do something. So Kelly says, Maybe Tony here could have a word with her."

"Kelly said that?"

"Right. Dickie says okay. He already found out where she lives. He gives me the address. Said her name's easy to remember. Corona, like the beer."

"And you had a word with her."

"Yeah. Look, buddy, she was never in danger. I had specific orders not to kill her."

"Never in danger?" I said.

"Right."

"You're a piece of work, Tony. How does Kelly know Dickie?"

"They met at some party in Beverly Hills, I think. Maybe a year ago. Dickie scores coke for him and sets him up with good-lookin' women. Hollywood types, California girls, you know? Kelly loves it. He probably has one of them three-hundred-pound hausfraus bitching at him back in Munich. So he keeps Dickie on the string by putting a little money in his investment deals."

"Name-recognition time," I said. "April Lennox."

"Don't know her," Tony said.

"A reporter from L.A. who got killed in Mexico."

"Not me, buddy. No way. All I do in Mexico is watch out for Kelly. Once in a while I give the cops some cash so we get in and out okay. I never killed nobody in Mexico."

"Sam Doyle," I said.

"Never heard of him. Really. I told you all I know about this. I'm just hired help."

I backed up toward the entrance door, holding my gun on him.

"Stay put for a while, Tony," I said. "When you get up, get out of Tucson. If I see you down here again, we won't have such a pleasant conversation."

"Plenty of work up in Phoenix," he said, a little too easily.

I reached behind me and opened the door. As I backed out and closed it, I heard him bumping around inside. I threw open the door and saw him struggling with his pants, around his ankles, reaching for something. His shins were close together and I fired one round at him as I slammed the door behind me. Tony screamed and clutched his right leg, just below the knee. Not much of a shot, I thought, but it got the job done. I ran to him and reached for his right ankle. He had an ankle holster and a small gun there. I pulled it out. Tony's face had gone white. I checked his wound and saw little blood.

"You won't bleed to death," I said. "Too bad."

I got the cell phone from his jacket and tossed it to him.

"Call whoever you call when things go south," I said. I backed out of the room again. On the way to my car, I threw Tony's gun into a dumpster. There was a pay phone by the office. I dropped in a quarter, dialed 911, and gave the operator the motel name and Tony's room number. "Shooting victim, not critical," I said, and hung up.

As I drove away, the hooker was back in business, climbing into another car on Miracle Mile.

CHAPTER 36

I RETURNED DAVID KATZ'S MERCEDES AND PICKED UP MY OWN CAR. David and his family were not home, so they didn't see my hands shaking or hear my heart pounding. I tried to remember the last time I had fired a gun in anger. On the Border Patrol, probably, and that had been years ago.

At my house, I poured a small glass of Cuervo Gold and drank it in a gulp. I started to pour another but good sense kicked in. I sat at the kitchen table and looked up the number for the executive terminal at Tucson International.

"Just wanted to be sure my friend Helmut Kelly got to his destination this morning," I said. "He chartered the Lear, six four Juliet." The jet's registration number ended in 64J. I had heard David Katz identify planes that way.

"Yes, sir," the woman on the phone said. "Sure did. Touched down SMO at eleven-forty-two."

"Thanks a lot," I said. SMO had to be Santa Monica Municipal Airport, a favorite of private jetsters on L.A.'s west side. I made a note to confirm that later.

I was staring longingly at the Cuervo bottle when Gabi called.

"How's your day?" she said.

"If you're feeling sadistic and vengeful," I said, "I have a wonderful story for you."

"I'm not mad at you," she said.

"I met the guy you *are* mad at," I said. "His name is Anthony Cazzo, of Phoenix. His aftershave is just as bad as you said. And he's in a world of hurt right now."

"I love this story," Gabi said. "More, more."

I told her about Cazzo, Kelly, and the connection to Dickie.

"What pigs," she said. "Do you believe him, about not killing April?"

"He's the wrong guy for it in Nogales," I said. "When he goes down there, it's with Kelly. The last thing they want is to have the distinguished Herr Kelly identified with a suspected murderer. If they did it, I think they contracted it out."

"Well, as my old journalism prof used to say, who are these 'they' you keep talking about?"

"It could go two ways, Gabi. One is that Dickie wanted to hurt April and either asked Kelly to have it done, or Dickie arranged it himself. Or Kelly wanted it done because April was about to make very public trouble for Amistadt."

"I like Amistadt for this," she said. "Dickie's a puny cokehead pimp. We know that now. He could talk about killing people, but probably never do it. But Amistadt has a lot to lose, and the kind of resources to take out April and Ricardo Esposito and his girlfriend."

"Alma," I said.

"Yeah, and maybe more, for all we know."

"Is your data service back online yet?"

"No," she said. "I'll let you know when I get anything."

"Run a guy named Gustavo Larriva," I said. "He's the new *maquila* manager. They brought in Carl Brooks to deal with uppity workers. Let's see what Larriva's specialty is."

"Okay," Gabi said. "Watch yourself, Brink. You may have put Cazzo out of commission for a while, but those guys are rattlesnakes. There's probably another one behind a rock nearby."

I CALLED VICENTE AND ASKED FOR HECTOR. VICENTE CALLED back in five minutes and said Hector didn't want to use the phone. I should come to the restaurant in Nogales.

María was hostessing when I arrived. She gave me a hug, took my arm, and led me back to Hector. He sat in his usual place when I arrived. Some late lunch customers lingered, but none near him. Hector poured small glasses of tequila for both of us and pushed one across the table to me.

"Friendly help," I said.

"She's great," he said. "Everybody loves her. A real people person, you know?"

"I know," I said. "You ever run across a guy named Dickie Ungerlieder?"

"Doesn't sound local," he said, smiling.

"L.A.," I said.

"We don't supply California," he said. "Awkward business rivalries involved there."

"Helmut Kelly?"

"I know of him. We don't move in the same social circles, but I know who he is. Just another European here to screw the Mexicans again, as far as I'm concerned."

"How about Anthony Cazzo?"

"Nope."

"These guys may be connected to April Lennox's murder," I said. "I think it's all about Amistadt, which means Kelly. And Dickie pimps for Kelly and gets him drugs."

"Nothing wrong with that," Hector said.

"Come on, Hector. Help me out here."

"Sorry to drag you down here for nothing," he said. "I can give you one good rumor on Amistadt, though."

"Okay."

"There's been talk that they're bailing out. Close the *maquilas* or sell them. Take the jobs to Bangladesh or wherever people work for a nickel an hour. Word is that when Brooks got murdered, they got scared."

I thought about it. "That makes no sense," I said, "if they killed him."

"This may come as a shock to you," he said, "but sometimes, foreigners fuck up in Mexico."

ON THE WAY HOME, I STOPPED TO SEE GABI. SHE WAS IN THE LIVING room, listening to Linda Ronstadt sing love songs in Spanish.

"Just the man I want to see," she said. It should have been a cheery greeting, but she sounded tired and looked spent. "I have reams of data for you."

"Anything juicy?" I said.

"As a matter of fact, a couple of things you won't believe. I got on the news service after I talked to you. I not only found the press release on that ribbon-cutting at the *maquilas* in Nogales, I found the picture. I bet it's the one you saw. I'm a little creaky today, Brink. Go get my laptop, will you? It's in my bedroom."

I found the machine sitting on a small desktop that Gabi had used in her student days. It was still turned on, so I kept it open and carried it to her. She set it on her lap and said, "Move over here, and I'll show you. I already downloaded the stuff."

I moved a chair next to hers. She fiddled with the keys and the mouse pad. In a moment, the picture from Carl Brooks's office wall appeared on the laptop screen.

"Your boy," she said, pointing at a man in the first row, center. "Helmut Kelly, North American director for Amistadt, presided at the opening day events."

"Okay," I said. "This picture bugged me for a long time. But I didn't know anything about Kelly then. I wonder what it was."

"I think I know," she said. "I'm not sure what it means, but it could be ugly."

"What?"

"Look here," she said. "Back row, next-to-the-last guy on the left."

"I can barely see him," I said. "He's in shadow, and the guy in front is blocking him a little."

"Check the caption," Gabi said.

I looked at the list of names. *Rear, l to r,* it said. First was Señor Humberto Rosales, assistant operations director, Sonora Facilities, Nogales. And next to him, now recognizable in the shadow, stood Mr. Robert Lennox, chairman and CEO of Robert Lennox Global Industries, Los Angeles, California, and member of the Amistadt Board of Directors.

"Jesus, Gabi," I said.

"It gets worse," she said.

"How?"

"Kelly is on the board of Lennox's company. And when I cross-ran their names, they turned up on two other boards together. They're a regular interlocking directorate, those guys."

I felt ill. I leaned forward, closed my eyes, and put my hands to my temples. Gabi moved up in her chair and pulled my head to her shoulder.

Have you met the old man? Jon Cartwright had asked. April brought Dickie to the party *just to freak out her father.*

"April said the story somehow got more important to her. She found out that her father's company owned part of a *maquila*."

"But how could she connect that with Juan Doe?" Gabi said. "That was all she had at that point. A dead guy from Mexico who wanted to talk to her."

"He wanted to talk about oppression and murder, she told me. Worker exploitation was a specialty of hers. I'll bet she did a little more digging and found out about the murders of *maquila* workers. Then she might have discovered the Lennox stake in Amistadt."

"It was no secret," Gabi said. "I found it pretty quickly. She could have, too."

"Jon Cartwright said she had a passion for that kind of story," I said. "And she had this oddly distant relationship with her father. If she made a connection . . ."

"There's no way you could have kept her out of Mexico," Gabi said.

"He could have ordered an autopsy in the States, but he didn't," I said, not looking up. "He told me that he'd work his big deal contacts in Washington and Sacramento. He never got back to me."

Gabi smelled of something fresh and clean, a faint hint of citrus blossom. Her skin was warm. I sat straighter and took her good hand in mine. I thought about the grief grid, the newsroom chart that plotted a child's death as life's worst moment.

"This can't be what it looks like," I said.

"How about that?" Gabi said. "I'm getting more cynical than you."

"She was his daughter," I said. "If he wanted her out of the way, he could have given her a house in Tahiti or an apartment in Paris."

"From what I know about her, she doesn't seem like the type to be bought off."

"I have to think about this, Gabi. I can't believe that Lennox was part of it. Maybe the henchmen in Mexico just got out of control."

"Well," she said, "let me give you one more little nugget, before I forget. It probably has nothing to do with April, but I ran the new plant manager's name, Gustavo Larriva?"

"Yeah."

"Gustavo has an interesting history. He managed an Amistadt plant in the Dominican Republic. It was closed and he moved to Juárez. About a year after he got there, the *maquila* closed. Amistadt shifted the work to the Philippines. It looks to me like Mr. Larriva's strong suit is boarding up Amistadt factories."

"That fits with something Hector told me."

"I have to take a nap, Brink. I'm just bone-deep weary from all this. Call me tomorrow, okay?"

"Tomorrow's Sunday," I said. "I think I'll be out of town."

CHAPTER 37

I THOUGHT OF GABI'S MOTHER, TELLING THE PILOT NOT TO GO TOO fast. This flight seemed supersonic, perhaps because I did not want to be where I was going. But we touched down, and I went through the familiar ritual with Hertz, and got on the 405, and turned east on Santa Monica, heading straight for Beverly Hills.

On a Sunday morning, early, I figured to have the best chance of catching Robert Lennox. There would be no penetrating his guard of security and secretaries at work, but I had already seen him answer his own door at home.

I parked on the street, as I had before, and took the long walk on flagstone steps to the house. I rang the bell and waited. I rang again. Something stirred in the front hallway, and Robert Lennox opened the door. He looked no better than he had when I saw him the first time.

"I knew you'd come back," he said. He stood aside and motioned me in. He wore a dark blue sweat suit and house slippers today. He led me through the big empty hallway and back to an office. It was a man's room, all dark wood paneling and bookcases, burgundy leather, and a great rosewood partners' desk near the east wall.

"Would you like a drink?" he asked. I shook my head, no.

"Well, I'll certainly have one," he said. He poured from a Glenfiddich bottle with a red number "40" on the label. Forty-year-old scotch at nine o'clock on a Sunday morning in a vast empty house.

I sat at the end of a large leather sofa. Lennox took a chair opposite me. He drank about half his ration of scotch and put down the glass.

"The other private detectives just wanted to climb on the gravy train," he said. "When I told them no for the second or third time, they went away. You never called again, but I knew you would be here."

"What happened?" I said.

"I don't know," he said. "You probably don't believe me, but I don't know."

"You're right," I said. "I don't believe you."

He started to reach for the whiskey glass, but he sat back and put his hands in his lap.

"I knew that April had been killed in Nogales, and I knew that Amistadt had business there. In fact, I was actually there once for an opening ceremony. But I hardly thought of the place since. I never made a connection. My friend Helmut Kelly runs his company, Amistadt, and I run mine. We're on each other's boards, but you know how boards of directors are."

"No," I said. "I don't."

"We essentially sign off on the CEO's plans. That's the way I want it in my company, and I naturally respect Helmut's wish to run his."

"That's just standard corporate malfeasance. How did your daughter get murdered?"

"Amistadt in Nogales was having serious cost control problems. The Mexican government was pressing for wage increases. They want to raise the pay in Mexico so fewer people will emigrate to the United States. They think that if illegal immigration eases, the U.S. will provide more trade benefits to Mexico."

"What does this have to do with April?" I said.

Now he finished the scotch. "Helmut and I were talking by phone one night. Late night here, morning in Munich. He said that some employees and outsiders were making trouble, demanding even more money, agitating the workforce. I'd had a couple of these." He held up his glass. "I said to him, Well, get rid of them. I meant fire the workers and buy off the outsiders. But I think he took me literally. He had to have thought about it before, of course, but perhaps what I said provided confirmation for him. I think he began to have some people, uh, eliminated. And he must have believed that he still had carte blanche to do that when April began investigating Amistadt."

"But he wouldn't kill your daughter, would he?"

"Of course not. But you understand how things work in large companies. Well, perhaps you don't. Someone told him that a reporter was being troublesome. He simply gave the order, not knowing who the reporter was. And the subordinate probably didn't even know that I'm a board member or that April was my daughter."

I stood up. I wanted some of that scotch for myself.

"Who was the subordinate?" I asked.

"That man Brooks, I suppose," Lennox said. "The manager there in Nogales. When he was murdered, I realized that Helmut must have other, dirtier people working for him."

"Sam Doyle?" I said.

"I have heard the name," he said. "I couldn't tell you exactly what he does."

I walked around the room, looking at the pictures of Lennox with presidents and governors, prime ministers and at least one king that I recognized.

"Are they closing those *maquilas* in Nogales?" I said.

"As I told you, I don't follow the day-to-day details of Amistadt's operation. But I imagine so, fairly soon. The wage differential is too great. Leaving Mexico for India or China now has almost the same value as leaving the U.S. for Mexico had years ago."

I looked on the walls and on his desk for a picture of April. There was nothing.

Behind me, Lennox said, "Are you a violent man, Mr. Brinker?"

I did not answer.

He said, "Those other detectives who came to me seemed to have a potential for violence. I sensed short tempers in them, and perhaps even a pleasure in taking violent action. I didn't see that in you."

"I shot a man in Tucson yesterday," I said.

"To death?" he asked in an eerily businesslike tone.

"No," I said, "but he probably deserved it. He'll kill someone someday."

"I've already killed someone, in a way," he said. "Do I deserve death?"

I returned to my place on the sofa. I ran my hand over the armrest.

"I have an old sofa," I said. "Not a great luxurious piece like this, but it's sturdy. It lasted three generations so far. It's worn on the end here, where all us Brinker men have rested our heads over the years."

Lennox looked blankly at me.

"April saw it and I told her about my father, and how when I saw the worn spot on the sofa, I could almost feel his short, bristly hair on my hand. She cried. She tried to fight it, but she actually cried. She slept on that sofa and clung to that spot through the night."

If I had slugged him or shot him, he could not have looked more stricken. He sank back in his chair.

In barely more than a whisper, he said, "Was that your answer to my question?"

"Death will get you, no matter what I do," I said.

"Yes," he said. "True enough. Frankly, I'm more worried about the life between now and then."

"Goodbye, Mr. Lennox," I said.

CHAPTER 38

GABI HAD GIVEN ME THE KEY TO HER APARTMENT. SHE ASKED ME TO pick up the mail, water two plants, and bring her an extra pair of jeans and two lightweight blouses. She lived in Marina del Rey, about halfway between Santa Monica Bay and the boat basins. Her apartment complex appeared to be filled entirely with energetic, handsome people like herself. I could still see her, driving up the PCH, singing, "I love L.A.," before she got worked over by a professional leg-breaker.

She had called the apartment manager to let him know that I was coming. I stopped at the office and introduced myself. He pointed me to the elevator and said Gabi's apartment was about halfway down the hall, facing the beach.

I let myself in and looked around. The old cop instinct took over. I checked for signs of break-in or searches. Everything was fine. The glass sliding door was shut tight and locked. I opened it and breathed in fresh air from the bay. It was cool at midday, nothing like Tucson. No wonder she wanted lighter clothing. I found the plants and watered them as instructed. The mail would be at the central delivery boxes in the lobby. I would get it on the way out.

I pushed open Gabi's bedroom door. It felt sneaky to walk in there, staring at everything, even though she had directed me to her closet. Beaten up or not, she had made her bed before she left.

Her closet was what I expected from a young career woman. Neat, nothing too fancy, lots of utilitarian matching colors. There was one slinky-looking black dress that I had never seen her wear. I found the jeans and the blouses, tucked them in a tote bag from the closet floor, and started to leave.

The pictures on her bedside table caught my eye. There were two. Jesús and Josephina Corona with Gabi in her UA graduation gown. McKale Center, the basketball arena and commencement ceremony venue, was in the background. Other grads and families milled on the edges of the photo, out of focus. Gabi was beaming that improbably wide and radiant smile that comes so naturally to college girls. Her parents looked proud, the kind of pride that makes you want to cry happily and hug everyone in sight.

The other picture showed Gabi and me, sitting at the foot of "A" Mountain on Fourth of July night. We were watching the annual fireworks show. I was fourteen and she was twelve.

My father took the shot, I think, and it was a lovely piece of amateur's luck. In the background, a pyrotechnic burst sent trails of red, white, and blue light across the sky. Gabi had raised her hands to her mouth in amazement, with a smile that foreshadowed her graduation day ten years later. She was watching the fireworks. I was watching her, and smiling, too.

CHAPTER 39

VICENTE AND I SAT IN U-NEEDA-BEBIDA, WHERE SAL GARCIA HAD invited me to the riot. It was early Monday afternoon. Only a couple of other customers had come in. They wore suits and ties, drank club soda, and checked their watches every five minutes. Lawyers, maybe, waiting for a jury verdict at the courthouse.

"I wouldn't mind finding this Kelly guy, rearranging his skeleton some, but Hector won't let me," Vicente said. "Whatever happens with the *maquilas,* he doesn't want his good name associated with it."

"He may be right," I said. "Nothing good is coming out of this."

"Word is," Vicente said, "nobody on the *maquila* floors even sees this guy Larriva anymore. He drives in, goes up to his office, hunkers down on the phone. He never comes out except to talk to the bookkeepers."

"They're going to shut it down," I said. "They're going to sneak out in the middle of the night in order to avoid facing anyone. They'll put some of the equipment in vans and steal away."

"That's about four thousand people with no jobs, man. Nogales can't handle that. That's no little recession. You're talking depression if that happens. Revolution in the streets."

"We should warn them," I said.

Vicente took a sip of beer and looked hard at me. "Whaddya talking about?" he said.

"I'm just saying we should get the word out. That might ratchet up the employee agitation level. And that might bring Kelly and his other muscle back to Mexico. I think that's Sam Doyle. I'd like to have both of them there."

"Well," Vicente said, "fine by me. But be sure you know what you're 'just saying' here, Brinker. You're putting those guys down there, right in the middle of four thousand pissed-off unemployed Mexicans. If you light the match, then somebody's gonna get burned."

"That could happen," I said.

WE STARTED WITH FRIDA AND MARÍA BUYING DRINKS FOR THEIR *maquila* friends at El Pájaro Rojo. Everyone knew that the women had dumped their assembly jobs to work for Hector, so they had money and nice clothes and a better place to live.

"It was easy to talk about," Frida told us the next morning. "People are worried about this for a long time already."

"Nobody was saying it's impossible?" I said.

"Oh, no," María said. "Two other *maquilas* already closed and sent jobs to some cheap country. So when we say we heard Amistadt is closing, it was all over the bar real fast."

"Some guys started telling us," Frida said. "Like they were the ones who had the secret, you know? But they heard it from people we told."

I said, "You want to go back tonight?"

"Sure," the women said at once.

Vicente peeled a handful of pesos off his roll of money and gave some to each woman.

"We should visit some other clubs, too," Frida said. "Not everyone goes to El Pájaro Rojo."

"I have a soft spot for that one because it's where we met you two," Vicente said.

Frida and María laughed.

"*¡Mentiroso!*" Frida said. You liar.

"Are there some places where just the guys go for a beer after work?" I asked.

"Sure," María said. "I know all the places where the boys go."

"Pass the word to a few of them," I said.

THINGS WENT FASTER THAN WE EXPECTED. THE NEXT DAY, VICENTE began hearing about dissention on the Amistadt *maquila* floors. Employees kept asking their supervisors if what they heard was true. The supervisors knew nothing, so they denied everything, then went upstairs to ask Gustavo Larriva what was going on. Larriva said Amistadt planned no changes. But he spent even more time on the telephone, and a fly on the office wall said he became irritable.

That night, Frida and María brought a man to Vicente's apartment. When the guard called up from downstairs, Vicente said to me, "You'll love this."

The women came in, each one holding on to one arm of their guest. He looked embarrassed.

"This is Enrique Aragón," Frida said.

María said, "He is the brother of our friend Alma."

"Ricardo Esposito's sweetheart," I said.

Enrique Aragón said in confident English, "*Sweetheart* is a good word, sir. My sister was an angel and Ricardo was a decent, respectful boy. We hoped they would marry."

"I'm so sorry," I said. "But I think we're close to learning how your sister was killed."

"That is why I am here," he said. "My little friends here tell me that I may be able to help you. I work in Building Number Two."

"You can help," I said.

Vicente said, "Here's a cell phone, Enrique. I'll give you a battery charger before you go. Keep the phone turned on at all times. We'll tell you when to be ready and what to do."

TWO DAYS LATER, FAR SOONER THAN WE THOUGHT, THE RUMORS had reached critical mass. The day before, Gustavo Larriva had not come to work. His secretary had been given a Tucson cell number to call in case of emergency. By the end of the day, she was told to convene all the building managers for a nine o'clock meeting the next morning. She should also plan for a meeting of all employees at ten o'clock in the cafeteria.

"Ten o'clock, then," Vicente said. "That's when it hits the fan."

"Right," I said. "I'm going back up to Tucson tonight. I called the hotel where Kelly stayed last time, and he's back. So I want to stake out the place and see if Doyle is with him. It'll make life easier if we know what to expect tomorrow."

"Okay," Vicente said.

"You arrange for the driver?" I asked.

"Ready to go," he said.

"Good."

"Lemme ask you something, Brinker. What if you're wrong? What if Doyle didn't kill your April girl, or Alma and Ricardo? What if Kelly didn't order it?"

"You care?" I said.

"I don't have to care," Vicente said. "I do this shit for a living. You don't. It's like Hector said. You come down here when you want to be somebody else. You gonna be able to live with that other person when you go home?"

"I know who I'll be tomorrow," I said. "You bring the artillery."

"Okay, *jefe,*" he said.

I WATCHED THE HOTEL DRIVEWAY FOR THREE HOURS. NEITHER HELmut Kelly nor Sam Doyle showed. They probably were there, all right, hunkered down until the command performance in Nogales the next morning.

As I gave up and pulled out, my cell phone rang.

"Mr. Brinker?"

"Yes."

"This is Robert Lennox. I still have your card. That's how I got your number."

I said nothing. Lennox cleared his throat. "I found confirmation of some things you asked me about on Sunday," he said. "I'm sending it to your fax number. Will you have access to it tonight?"

"I'll be there in about fifteen minutes," I said.

"Good night, then," he said, and the line went dead.

I sped home. I made two passes around the block. If Doyle was in town, he might decide to visit me again. The house and street looked clean. When I let myself in, the alarm was still armed. I switched it off, reset it, and went to my office. Several printed pages sat in the out tray of my fax machine.

The first page was a handwritten cover sheet. "Mr. Brinker," it read, "I called the Amistadt offices in my capacity as a director, and then the commercial section of our Embassy in India. I hope this information is useful to you." It was signed simply, "RL."

I tossed the sheet onto my desk and read the next page. It was a copy of a press release from the Commercial Section of the United States Embassy in New Delhi. "The government of India and Amistadt, S.A., of Munich, Germany, have concluded agreements for five new assembly plants in New Delhi and Calcutta. The plants will produce a variety of high technology equipment, including cable telecasting connections and aviation control equipment. Approximately 4,000 positions will be created by Amistadt's investment, supplemented by grants from the government of India. Amistadt previously maintained these facilities in Nogales, Mexico. Operations will be transferred in approximately six months."

Lennox had scribbled in the margin, "This was released prematurely. Amistadt must keep this quiet to keep Nogales running for the transition period."

We had been ready to fake it, but this was the real deal. My heart pounded as I turned to the next page.

It was an interoffice memo from Hilda Frobe of the accounting office in München. That was Munich, I assumed. "Mr. Lennox, I am pleased to provide the information you requested by telephone today. The Amistadt Mexico records do indicate that three payments totaling 300,000 United States dollars were disbursed from this office in the last year to Mr. Samuel Doyle. The expenditures were approved directly by Herr Kelly for security operations. This money was deposited directly to Mr. Doyle's account in Zurich. If I may be of further assistance in any matter, please contact me."

A hundred thousand dollars, three times, to Doyle. Frau Frobe's memo did not give dates, but I had no doubt that Doyle's fees were paid soon after the deaths of Alma Aragón, Ricardo Esposito, and April Lennox.

CHAPTER 40

Kelly surprised us with his pretense of magnanimity. The Amistadt cafeteria was too small to accommodate the entire workforce from five *maquila* buildings. The company hired a video production company from Tucson to run a closed-circuit presentation from the cafeteria to all other buildings. They even installed a television at the guard post. Overnight, Amistadt used its clout and bribery budget to get two trucks full of electronic equipment through Mexican customs and onto the *maquila* property. By the time Kelly and Larriva stepped onto the makeshift stage at ten o'clock, they could be seen by every Amistadt employee in Nogales.

And by Vicente and me, sharing a bottle of tequila and a TV monitor with the guard at the main entrance.

Larriva introduced Helmut Kelly. Polite applause greeted him, but not much. He stood at a solitary microphone stand, not a podium, looking confident and commanding in a dark blue, two-thousand-dollar suit.

"My friends and colleagues," he said, in pretty good Spanish, "thank you for coming and for listening to me this morning." Then he switched to English. Larriva stepped up to translate each sentence.

"I am aware of many rumors about the future of our company in Nogales. I have come here today to tell you that these rumors are false and malicious. There is no plan—let me repeat that—there is no plan to close these facilities or to eliminate one job."

A few people clapped, then Larriva translated and the entire cafeteria crowd applauded. Watching on his monitor, our friend the guard nodded approvingly and grinned.

"Tengo cuatro niños," he said. I have four children.

Kelly was saying, "These vicious rumors are disruptive. All of us at Amistadt understand how upset you must be. That is why I have come this far, why I have interrupted business in Europe, to fly here and assure you that your hard work will be rewarded. Your jobs are safe!"

Now he had them roaring, stomping their feet, cheering, clapping. He held up his hands to quiet the ovation.

"And now, my dear friends, to set your minds even more at ease if necessary, I will gladly answer any questions that you may have about these rumors or about our true plans."

The crowd was silent.

"It's just like in school," Kelly said, "waiting for the first brave student to volunteer."

The workers in the cafeteria laughed. Our guard said, "If I

were in there, I'd ask him for a raise for everyone." Kelly was winning them over. I started to wonder if we could pull this off.

Then we heard a muffled voice from somewhere in the big room. The camera panned around and zoomed in on a man who had stood, holding a packet of papers in his hand. Someone from the video crew ran up with a microphone and held it for the man to speak.

Enrique Aragón said in English, "Sir, may I ask you to explain the press release from the United States Embassy in New Delhi, India, reporting that all work at this *maquiladora* will be moved to new facilities in India?"

A few bilinguals in the crowd murmured. Kelly was struck dumb. He stood there at his microphone, staring at Aragón with a mix of shock and hatred. Alma's brother switched to Spanish and repeated his question. I could hear the gasps where I stood, straight from the cafeteria building, without the aid of the TV monitor.

Finally, Kelly said, "That is utterly false. There is no such information." Larriva anxiously translated. The crowd looked toward Enrique Aragón.

"Sir," Aragón said in Spanish, "there is a computer at the wall to your right. Amistadt has kindly provided it for employee use during our lunch hours. It is connected to the Internet. You do not have to take my word. If you will choose any person in this room who speaks English and Spanish, and ask that person to locate the Commercial Section of the U.S. Embassy in India Web site, we will see and hear if there is such an information."

Aragón had spoken quietly, letting the microphone amplify his words and authority. Everyone in the room knew that his sister, a labor activist, had been murdered. Probably they all knew about Ricardo Esposito. The video crew's microphones now picked up no sound but the cafeteria's droning air conditioner. No one spoke. No one even seemed to breathe. Every face in the room was turned toward Helmut Kelly. He spoke quickly to Larriva, then wheeled around and stalked to a rear door.

"Señor Kelly must leave now for urgent business," Larriva said. "Once again, these rumors are utterly false." But his words were drowned out by angry jeers from the *obreros*. They recognized a trapped liar when they saw one. A few men raced toward the door where Kelly had exited.

The video screen went dark, but Vicente and I knew what was coming next. A black Cadillac sedan screeched around from behind the cafeteria building and headed for the exit.

Vicente gave the guard a hundred-dollar bill and said, "Take your lunch break, now, *amigo*. Downtown." He pulled a gun from his jacket. The guard got the message and scurried off to Avenida Obregón. Vicente and I ducked down out of sight in the little shack.

"I thought Hector didn't want you in on this," I said.

"He said, 'I'll deny any knowledge of your actions, Mr. Phelps.' Then he gave me a cigar and said, '*Buena suerte.*'"

The Cadillac bore down on the exit, its horn blaring for the guard to open the gate. As the car approached the chain-link fence, the driver hit the brakes. He jumped out, leaving his door open, and screaming Spanish obscenities into the guard shack.

Vicente ran to the driver, faked a hard punch into his stomach, and winked as the man went down and rolled out of the car's path. In another instant, Vicente jumped in on the driver's side and I yanked open the passenger door. We pointed our guns at the men in the back seat. Kelly looked ready for a massive coronary, and Sam Doyle's hand stopped halfway to the shoulder holster under his jacket.

"Aloha again," I said.

"You dumb shit," he said. "You'll never get out of this town. We own every cop between here and the border crossing."

Vicente laughed. "I think we might have topped your offer," he said. "Look out there."

A police officer on a motorcycle pulled up to the guardhouse. He walked through, pushed the button that opened the gate, then remounted his bike and waved for us to follow. I hit the child protective lock switch to prevent anyone in the back seat from opening the doors. We glided down Avenida Obregón.

Doyle said, "I'd love to see you drive this across. You'll have a good old Homeland Security SWAT team on your sorry ass before you know what hits you."

"Who said anything about going across?" I said.

The motorcycle cop pulled into an alley. He turned and waved, then sped off. Vicente stopped the Cadillac and turned around.

"Before the crowd from the factory arrives, Mr. Brinker would like to ask you a couple of questions."

Helmut Kelly began to shake like a man with malaria. Doyle smirked.

"Alma Aragón, Ricardo Esposito, April Lennox," I said. "You did them all, didn't you?"

"You couldn't prove I ever met those people," he said.

"I could prove you got three hundred thousand dollars," I said. "Nice convenient installments, right after each murder."

Doyle stopped smiling.

"Didn't you get paid for doing Brooks?" I said.

"That pathetic wimpy chicken farmer," Doyle said. "I'd have done him for free."

Vicente said, "I think Herr Kelly just crapped his pants. The smell's pretty nasty in here." He put down the driver's window. We could hear a roar in the distance, growing louder.

I said, "We have people in the crowd telling them about the murders. They always suspected it was a company job anyway. Kelly, the guy who braced you in the meeting was Alma Aragón's brother. I wouldn't give much for your credibility with those people right now."

Kelly was sobbing, big deep wails and shakes of his upper body that made the Cadillac rock a bit. We could hear the crowd getting closer.

"We'll be leaving you now," I said.

"Brinker," Doyle said. His face bore no rage or fear, only meanness and an ugly pleasure in it. "That April Lennox was some piece of ass. We tied her up, but she still bucked like a little bronco. I wish I could have kept her for a few days."

I raised my gun and leaned into the back seat. I felt my hand tightening on the trigger. I could anticipate the sound of the shot and the pleasure of watching Sam Doyle drop out of this life.

Vicente touched my arm gently and said, "You've gotta live after this. He's dead anyway."

I kept the gun pointed at Doyle's forehead. A drum beat in my head and my vision turned crimson.

Doyle laughed and said, "You don't have the fuckin' guts."

Vicente said, "Five seconds, tops, *amigo,* or the crowd gets us, too."

I pulled back my gun and pushed open the door. Vicente hit the lock button on his side, jumped out, and slammed the door shut. We ran down the alley just as the first line of the mob raced along Avenida Obregón and spotted the Cadillac. We were turning the corner, not daring to look back, as the mob poured into the alley. We heard pounding sounds, wood on metal, wood on glass, angry shouts. There came a sound like "whoosh," as if all the air had been sucked out of a small area.

"Crowd's well equipped," Vicente said. "I wonder how that happened."

In a moment, cheers rose behind us. We never heard a scream. But as we doubled back to the Avenida, we saw black smoke in the alley.

"Burned alive," Vicente said. "Pretty fair punishment for murdering three or four people to pump up your profit."

I just shook my head. To the south, more fires burned. Smoke rose in five growing plumes from Amistadt, the international city of friendship.

CHAPTER 41

THE TUCSON TELEVISION STATIONS LED WITH IT THAT NIGHT. TWO of them had no real video, just lame aftermath shots of the charred Cadillac and the burned-out *maquila* complex. One station had pictures of two covered bodies being wheeled into the local coroner's office. A clock in the background said three o'clock. That was three hours after the car fire was extinguished. Vicente and I figured that the cops must have reenacted that scene for a few pesos.

One station apparently made a deal with the video service that ran the closed-circuit show. That channel showed the meeting, Enrique Aragón's challenge, Kelly's hasty exit. Nobody had the Cadillac's stop at the gate, or its detour to the alley.

"Customs will have its own video at the U.S. entry," Vicente said. "They'll have you and me coming into Arizona."

"So we just came down to shop," I said. "I buy prescription

pain pills there all the time. Totally legal. Nothing unusual."

The crowd had tried to storm into the United States, but Homeland Security ordered the border closed about five minutes after Vicente and I walked through. The two Nogales crossings were fortified with Border Patrol agents, Customs officers, marksmen from the Joint Narcotics Counteroffensive Task Force, and Arizona Department of Public Safety officers.

Kelly and Doyle were identified as an executive and an employee of Amistadt. Police said it was not clear how their car caught fire, but a rigorous investigation was already under way. One State Judicial Police commander said the Cadillac was not assembled in Mexico, so it might have been of inferior quality.

An Amistadt spokesman in Munich confirmed that the Mexican operation would be moved to India. He said the home office had not yet conveyed that information to Herr Kelly at the time of the *maquila* meeting. That surely was why Kelly had inadvertently misspoken. He did not mention, and no journalist noted, that Herr Kelly pretty much *was* the home office.

After the news, Vicente stood up and finished his beer. I walked him to the door.

"Going to see one of your Tucson sweeties?" I asked.

"No," he said. "I promised Frida and María I'd be home tonight."

"Give them my love," I said.

"Give it yourself," he said. "I could use some reinforcements."

"Another time, Vicente."

"Sure," he said. We shook hands and he headed off to Mexico.

Dolores called from New York. She said, "I just saw the satellite feed from Tucson. It has the *maquilas* burning in Nogales."

"You should have been there," I said. "You'd have won an Emmy."

"Don't tell me *you* were there," she said. "I saw that it was Amistadt, but I didn't think . . . I don't know what I didn't think."

"It's the end of the April Lennox case," I said. "We got some justice in a crude way."

"Were you there when those men died?" Dolores asked.

"Nearby," I said.

A pause, and then, "I don't want to ask you anything else about it."

"All right," I said.

"Things are happening here," she said. "A promotion, I'm pretty sure. Maybe even the network. They still do real news there, usually."

"I'm glad for you," I said.

"There's always going to be a Mexico, Brink, wherever you are."

"Well, then," I said, "I'll have to be careful."

"Me, too," she said.

At ten o'clock, I was in the living room, lying on the old sofa. I had started the last bottle of McManis cabernet. Emmylou Harris sang a mournful ballad about peace at Arlington. It occurred to me that I did not know where April Lennox was buried. I'll have to find out, I thought. I'll go over there and stand by her grave and tell her that it's done.

When the doorbell rang, I didn't bother to check the security camera. I realized as I opened the door that I had been stupid and careless, but standing there was Gabi Corona.

"I suppose 'Light My Fire' would be a bad joke tonight, huh?" she said.

"The Doors, 1967," I said. "Come on in."

She walked without apparent pain and plopped down on the sofa. Her eye bruise was lighter and the swelling on her lip was down. She picked up my wineglass and took a sip.

"Nice," she said. "Get yourself a glass, too."

I laughed and went to the kitchen. When I returned, she patted the sofa beside her. I sat there. Gabi put her head on my shoulder.

"The lip hasn't really healed yet," she said. "Don't worry."

"Okay," I said. I poured wine into my new glass.

"I should be mad at you," Gabi said.

"Why?"

"You knew the story of the year was about to pop, and you didn't tell me."

"No place for someone with sore bones and a cast on her wrist," I said. "I got out with about two seconds to spare. You've paid enough for my sins."

"Can I lie down here?" she said.

"Sure."

She swung around and lay with her legs across mine and her head on the worn armrest.

"It looks like a piece of the leather was cut out here," she said.

"Yes," I said. "I have something I want to do with it."

Gabi probably figured that if I wished to tell her, I would have. She looked up at me and said, "When you were in my apartment, getting those blouses for me, did you see the picture in my bedroom?"

"I liked it. I remember the day."

"Me, too. I love that picture. I did from the day your father gave it to me. He could see how I felt about it. The next day, he came back to the house and gave Papa the negative. Papa made some copies and put them in his safe-deposit box. One day last year, I told him how faded that picture was getting. So he got out one of the copies and gave it to me. And he told me about the negative. He said, 'If you're careful, *querida,* you'll always have memories that matter.'"

"He's right," I said.

"I told Papa that I can get it scanned. I'll have a perfect digital master copy forever. He thinks that's amazing."

"They're wonderful people, Gabi."

She said, "I didn't really need the blouses."

CHAPTER 42

ON A COLD JUNE MORNING, THE SKY GRAY AND HEAVY WITH LOW clouds, I stood on a green ridge in San Diego County. It was imaginatively landscaped with trees and hedges to block the view and noise of the bustling coastal highway below. But from this spot, one could see the beach and waves, and the ocean to the horizon on a kinder day. Robert Lennox had told me that April chose the place herself after burying a young friend there.

The gravestones all lay flat on the ground. Some had urns that could be raised to hold flowers on birthdays and holidays. I read April's stone. Just her name and her dates of birth and death. She was twenty-seven when she died.

I sat next to the marker. The grass was wet. We were alone on that ridge.

"I know you didn't like cops much, but I think you'll understand this," I said. "A homicide detective came to my school when

I was a little boy. It was job day, I guess, and he was representing the police department. He told me something I've remembered ever since. He said that he tried to solve cases so the people who cared about the victim would know what happened. Well, people cared about you. And now we know what happened. It's not all we wish, but it's what we could do for you."

A breeze came up, damp but gentle, carrying a faint sound of surf from the beach below.

"I brought you something," I said. I took it from my pocket. It was about two inches long and an inch wide. It would probably look like an old, fallen leaf when I placed it here. I pushed it deep into the soft earth between the edge of the stone and the grass, where it would hold fast and not be caught by the mowers or the wind. It was still supple, despite its age, and it seemed to fold comfortably into its new home.

The clouds lowered. The wind subsided. Mist formed. Rain would follow soon. I stood and looked down at April's name and my small gift.

"Hang on to that," I said. "I'm sorry I didn't help you when I could, April. I'm sorry that I didn't know you better."

I turned away to start the journey home. After a few steps, I stopped and looked back. I said to her, "My loss."

AUTHOR'S NOTE

This story is fiction, but parts of it are rooted in reality. Dozens of young women have indeed been murdered in a Mexican border town. The real killings happened in Ciudad Juárez, Chihuahua, not Nogales, Sonora, where the crimes in this novel occur. As I write, the Juárez murderers have not been identified with certainty. This likely will remain true even if suspects are convicted.

For information about workaday life at the *maquiladoras* in Nogales, I am indebted to the outstanding journalism of John Dougherty and David Holthouse of the *Phoenix New Times.* I learned about the seldom-seen historic art and the restoration of Mission San Xavier del Bac from the work of anthropologist Bernard L. Fontana and photographer Edward McCain in *Arizona Highways.*

Kris Pickel of KOLD-TV in Tucson produced a gutsy, award-winning report on the real Fourth Avenue riot; I thank her for sharing the videotape.

Don Haight gave me Gabi's California freeway sign. Kevin O'Connell came up with the music game.

I am especially grateful, again, to Hope Dellon, my editor, and Esmond Harmsworth, my agent, for their invaluable advice and support.

As always, Marianne Mitchell spoke the Spanish. If any of it went wrong in these pages, *es culpa mía*.